VARDØGER

VARDØGER

Stephen Volk

VARDØGER

First published in 2009 by Gray Friar Press.
9 Abbey Terrace, Whitby,
North Yorkshire, YO21 3HQ, England.

Email: gary.fry@virgin.net
www.grayfriarpress.com

Typesetting by Gary Fry

ISBN: 978-1-906331-14-6

You have to do things on impulse sometimes. Got to do things on impulse now and again.

The sign ahead read "Shewstone House Hotel," in that ornate English script normally reserved for the titles of Jane Austen films, gold lettering on National Trust green, proudly displaying its four AA stars. *They probably get that for there being a kettle in the room, or a Corby trouser press,* thought Sean. There he was, being negative again. And that's what he didn't want to be, not this weekend. This was supposed to be a nice weekend. That was the whole point. Get out of the heaviness and grime of London. Leave your troubles way behind you. Rest, fresh air, clean sheets, beds made by some total stranger, and a little bit of how's your father if he was lucky.

The courtesy mini-bus slowed down, turned and entered between two suitably moss-encrusted pillars topped by eagles, or was it griffins? Sean didn't get a good enough look. Through the rear window the big gates closed automatically as if pushed by invisible, servile hands

"Leaves on the track. Wrong sort of snow. Something like that," he said. "Still it gave us more time to enjoy the trolley service. Every cloud has a silver lining, know what I mean?"

The driver laughed as they rode down a long, oak-lined avenue which was pretty inadequately described by the word driveway.

"Anyway. Thanks for waiting. Cheers."

"No problem, sir. That's what they pay me for."

Sean smiled at his wife. The sun, streaming in, did good things to Alison's gushing blond hair, making her

1

look like someone off a sixties Athena poster, gossamer-thin summer skirt, massive sunglasses and espadrilles, breast-bone highlighted over the low U of her T-shirt with an exclamation mark of perspiration.

"Even the railway station looks nice out here." Sean said loudly in order for the driver to hear over the engine. "I half expected Jenny Agutter and Bernard Cribbins to be there waving at us." He chuckled at his own joke.

"Know what you mean, sir. Not quite, sir."

Ali elbowed Sean in the ribs. *What?* He dropped his smile like a brick, took her hand in his. He squeezed it, widened his grin and followed her gaze back out of the windshield ahead, at the looming frontage of the hotel.

"Blimey O'Reilly…"

The photo on the internet hadn't done it justice. Sean felt his heart beating a little faster. It was pathetic. Some deep social inferiority awakened in his DNA. *Bollocks.* But it *was* stunning. History seeped out of its pores. Births, deaths, murders, mayhem. *Shagging, no doubt. Generations of it, no doubt.* As they approached he could see the Victorian and later embellishments including a swimming pool and conservatory. *This is the business, this is,* he thought. *God, Americans would wet their knickers over this. Talk about* Remains of the Day. *Talk about* Gosford Park. *Shit a brick.* Then, strangely, he thought of how much his mum and dad would be intimidated by a place like this, but sod that, he wasn't them, he was going to enjoy this. These people were going to be serving him, not vice versa. He patted Ali on the knee, excited as a little kid.

The gravel crunched under the tyres as the mini-bus pulled up outside the tastefully discreet arrow pointing to reception. As Sean climbed out, taking in the fenestration open-mouthed, Ali looked behind her at a line of parked Volvos, BMWs, and assorted four wheel drives.

2

"Modest little residence," murmured Sean, cricking his neck.

"Yeah. On a clear day you can see the poor people," said Alison, equally *sotto voce*, scanning the endless lawns at the moment being manicured by a gardener in rolled-up shirt-sleeves phutting along on his motorized mower. The geezer raised a hand of greeting before doing a brisk U-turn.

"Do you think they need some plastering done?" said Sean. "I can always leave my card."

"Don't you dare show me up."

"Shame on you. I thought you were proud of your working class roots."

"Yeah… not *that* proud."

"Welcome to Shewstone House." The driver in his slate grey chauffeur outfit and peaked cap had placed their luggage next to them.

"Thanks. Thanks a lot, mate. Er…" Sean searched his pockets for a tip, but by the time he had, the driver had got back in the mini-bus and was reversing.

"Damn."

"Every pound a prisoner," said his wife.

"What do you mean?"

She kissed him on the lips. "I'm winding you up. I don't think he was expecting anything. He probably earns more than you do."

"Oh, thanks."

She gurned a wicked grin at him, picked up their bags.

"Hold on. Leave that, love. Some flunkey'll do that. That's what they're here for. Remember?"

"Sean. I do *not* need some flunkey to carry my bags."

Sean negotiated the revolving doors with a suitcase in each hand, and a bag under each armpit. He went bandy-legged by the weight of it all, Norman Wisdom-like. The look on Ali's face was one he knew of old. *Yes, but you love me really, don't you?* And of course – bloody fool that he was, pack mule that he was – he did. They reached the reception desk and he plonked them down in a Tower of Pisa.

"So," he whispered, "D'you think they'll know we got this on special offer with those vouchers?"

"Oh yeah," said Ali. "From the tattoos across our foreheads. What are you like? For all they know, you could be one of those eccentric millionaires or something. You know, the scruffy type."

"Scruffy type? You…" He tweaked her ribs with hands like crab claws. A chubby, terminally provincial girl turned from the fax machine with a cloyingly disingenuous chirpiness normally found only within the confines of building society commercials.

"Hello there, sir, madam. How can I help you?"

"Oh. Hi. It's Mr and Mrs Merritt," said Sean. "We're booked in for two nights? Friday and Saturday, tonight and tomorrow."

While the girl smilingly went to her computer display screen, Ali removed her sunglasses and rotated, absorbing the Tudor baronial decor.

"What do you reckon then?" said Sean out of the corner of his mouth.

"I don't mind slumming it."

They grinned at each other like school kids, then admonished each other wordlessly and went all po-faced. This was way beyond expectations, and secretly they wanted to jump up and down, stupidly, but a little bit of decorum was in order. After a few seconds, the girl came back from her computer screen, wiping her nose with a tissue.

"What was the name again, sir?"

"Merritt. M... E... double-R... I... double-T."

"Sorry. OK... OK, I see. If you'd like to take a seat out on the terrace a minute? I'll just..."

"There's not a problem, is there?"

"No, no, no. I'm sure there isn't. You're just not showing on the, ah, computer, Mr Merritt."

"I phoned at least three weeks ago."

"Right. Oh, right, er. Do you remember who you spoke to?"

"No. I didn't ask their name."

"Did they tell you to send confirmation in writing?"

"Yes. And I did. I wrote a letter. I've got a copy of it but I didn't think it was necessary to bring it."

Ali could see him getting agitated. She knew the signs. "It's all right," she said under her breath. "Relax."

"Are you sure it was for tonight, sir? The tenth?"

His lips, a straight line, started to go white. "Yes. Of course I am."

A smooth young assistant manager appeared, a dark, bland suit containing a light bland person. "What's the problem, Karen?"

The receptionist straightened her back. "Gentleman says he's booked in for tonight and tomorrow night, but he's not on the computer and we're fully booked, what with the wedding and – "

"What?" Now Sean was teetering on the brink of alarm.

"If you can just bear with us, sir," said the assistant manager. "I'm sure we can sort this out. If you'd just like to take a seat on the terrace..."

"No, I would not like to take a seat on the terrace. I'd like to take a seat in my *room*."

5

Ali said, "Sean, don't, God."

Passing hotel guests down-turned their crepe mouths and looked offended by this disruption to their oasis of calm, and that made Sean all too aware of becoming loud. *This isn't loud*, he thought. *I can show them LOUD.* The moon-faced girl was back at the VDU screen. It reflected in her glasses. At first he'd thought she was quite attractive but she wasn't. At all.

"Sir? Sir... Here we are. I see now... There's a booking here for Mr Merritt, a double room with bathroom ensuite..."

Sean sighed with relief.

"...booked for Friday the third and Saturday the fourth. That's... ah, that's *last* weekend, sir."

Ali turned her back to the desk and shut her eyes. Sean leaned his elbows onto it, doing his superhuman best to keep within the limits of non-berserkness. It was a tall, tall order. Getting taller by the second.

Calm. "Are you telling me I'm not booked in for tonight and tomorrow night?"

"You were here last weekend, sir."

Calm, calm. "I'm here now."

"According to the computer you were here last weekend, sir. You paid your bill."

"No, no, no. Somebody *else* stayed here, obviously. Somebody *else* paid the room bill and there's been a mistake with the name."

The girl turned to the assistant manager. "M... E... double-R... I... double-T." She said it like some esoteric code. They shared each other's blankness.

Sean decided to interrupt their communion with whatever ethereal spirits hotel staff commune with, and said slowly but forcefully, as if speaking to a small child, a small child whose first language was not English: "There – has – been – a – mistake."

The assistant manager stepped forward. "Did you pay this bill, sir?"

"I'm going mad. No. Are you listening? I wasn't *here* last weekend. I'm here *now*."

It was Ali's cue to but in. She was always the peacemaker. Some things never changed. "Look, it doesn't matter how it happened. But is there something you can do? What are we going to do if there are no rooms?"

"Hang on, hang on," said Sean. "This room was *booked*."

"Nice to see you back so soon, Mr Merritt! Glutton for punishment, eh, sir? Can't keep you away!"

Sean looked down at his hand which another man, the manager, an unctuous clown cut out of the same pie-dish as his pimply minion, was shaking violently, then gazed up at the man's face with a deeply-etched frown of mystification. The manager's smile slid off it like a slate from a roof. His grip went soft, then limp. Sean looked behind the desk at the Lego duo.

"Is – is he taking the…?" Then, after a moment, he laughed. He thought of the jokers he worked with. That prank his brother played at the wedding. Those TV shows where they set up members of the public. *Trigger Happy TV. Noel Edmonds, as was. Jeremy Beadle, as was. Never found him funny. Ant and bloody Dec.* "OK. What's going on here? Are two men dressed as enormous squirrels going to come out from behind that palm tree, or what?"

The manager wasn't laughing. "Is something wrong, Mr Merritt?"

"I was not here last weekend. I've never seen you before in my life, mate. I've never *been here* in my life."

"Sean. Calm down," said his wife.

7

The manager darted a nervous glance at Ali as if seeing her for the first time, his mind ticking over. Then he began to stammer.

"I – yes, I see," he said, flustered. "I'm so sorry, sir." He gave another semi-furtive glance at Ali. "I must be, ah, must be mistaking you for someone else, clearly. Of course I am." He blushed very slightly.

Ali sighed and tugged Sean's arm. She didn't enjoy embarrassment in others, whether they were in the right or in the wrong. It simply wasn't a field sport to her. She was also, unlike Sean, fairly tolerant, and believed that mistakes happen, and it's no good getting upset about it. While the poor man conferred in a huddle with his team, trying to sort things out, she pulled Sean away, escorting him out onto the terrace and dumping him in a big wickerwork armchair, where he simmered on a low heat for about fifteen minutes.

Around then a waitress cleared away the longstanding debris of a previous guest's afternoon tea of half-nibbled scones on willow-pattern plates. Ali smiled at her, as it was in her nature to do. Sean didn't. He was brooding. As was his nature to do, and do often.

"The perfect bloody start to a perfect bloody holiday, eh?"

"Don't worry," said Ali. "It doesn't matter."

"It does. The first time away, the two of us, for four years. It *does* matter."

She rubbed his knee, smiled a big smile, nodding for him to smile one back, go on, for him to say, *Hey, it'll be all right.* But he couldn't. He sighed. Pissed off. The gloom had descended. And while she hated it, she tolerated it. She was a tolerant person. She could see the manager appearing in the distance, looking round, and targeting them.

"Mr Merritt? Mrs Merritt? I think we've solved the big mystery, sir."

The assistant manager had a paper receipt in his hands. "Have you used your Visa card in the last few weeks, Mr Merritt?"

"I think so." Sean patted his pockets for his wallet. "I'm sure I have."

"You see," said the manager. "We have a signature, which explains why someone would have claimed to be you." Sean found his Visa card and laid it flat on the table in front of them. "Somebody must have made a copy of your card some time before last weekend, and used it here along with a fake signature"

The young one put the signed receipt next to Sean's Visa card, comparing them. "Did you make any other payments on the third and fourth, sir, do you know?"

"I... I don't know. I'll have to take a look at my next statement when I get it."

Ali said, "Damn. We should cancel it, and phone up that number, stop any more..."

"I will," said Sean. "I will do, give me a chance. I don't know, all sounds pretty farfetched to me. I mean..."

"Come on," said Ali. "Credit card fraud. You hear about it all the time. They get your details off the internet, or when your card is swiped at a petrol station, fake a new card, a new identity, spend your money and you never even know about it."

"Anyway," said the manager. "The good news is, we've had a cancellation. So we can offer you a room after all. Double. Ensuite."

Ali exhaled. "Thank God for that. We could see ourselves kipping the nearest bus shelter, couldn't we Sean? ...Sean?"

Sean had picked up the credit card receipt and was peering at his signature, comparing it to the one on his card. They were identical.

"Yes. We could."

Sean couldn't relax till he'd cancelled the card, telling the call centre (in Calcutta, it sounded like) that he thought it had been used fraudulently. They checked his purchases and there didn't seem to be anything unaccountable except the Shewstone House bill, so they reassured him he wouldn't be liable now he'd reported it and said he'd have a new card in five to ten days. *Job done. What was he worried about?* He chopped up his current card into tiny pieces using a pair of scissors from the reception desk drawer. After that the manager took a key from a hook as Sean signed the hotel registration form Ali had completed. "Thank you, sir. Giles will help you with your bags. And please accept a complimentary bottle of wine with your meal tonight, as a token of apology."

"Oh," Ali beamed perkily. "Thank you very much."

"Not at all, madam. Have a wonderful stay at Shewstone House. Sleep well."

Giles, an Australian student, took the cases, as loaded as Sean had been but with none of the attending effort. The boy was clearly in training for the 2012 Olympics. He had biceps like beach balls and veritably bounced up the wide oak staircase as Ali and Sean followed him to their room.

As they ascended into creaky, French-polished history, Sean heard the ratatat of the credit card pieces landing in a waste paper bin and looked back over his shoulder at the manager and assistant manager below.

10

They were standing like shop window dummies at the foot of the stairs, not looking at each other or even moving – as if both knew something that they were not about to let on.

"Look at these old photos, Sean."

He looked. The atrium of the staircase was covered in huge, dark, impressive Elizabethan oil paintings. *Photos.*

"Bit of a rogues gallery, isn't it?" said Giles.

The boards of the stairs protested underfoot as they ascended. A pigtailed little girl in her school uniform, bottle-green blazer outlined with a yellow trim, walked down the stairs past them. Sean smiled at her but she didn't smile back.

"Look," said Ali. "Henry VIII."

"Not quite," said Giles.

"He could do with signing up with Weight Watchers, whoever he is," said Sean.

"It's the family who lived here," said Giles. "Till the chain took over, that is."

"Gosh," said Ali. "All looking down at us…"

"Thinking, 'Who are these oiks trailing muck up my stairs?' " added Sean.

"Here, d'you think it's haunted?"

"It's creaky enough. Five stars in the Good Creak Guide, this place." Sean raised a visor and peeked inside the helmet of a fifteenth-century suit of armour. "Oi! Anybody at home?"

The pigtailed little girl in the school blazer who had just passed him came downstairs a second time, and this time she giggled, she thought he was being funny. Sean's eyes followed her and he did a quick double take as Giles carried the suitcases on, up, then ran to catch up, before he had too much time to think about what he'd seen, or thought he'd seen.

11

Giles entered Room 23 first, stacking the cases, switching on the two bedside lights and opening the bathroom door. The room was straight out of *World of Interiors*. A large ornate mirror virtually covered one wall. Suddenly struck by an afterthought, Sean dug in his pocket and gave Giles a tip.

"Thank you, sir. Enjoy your stay."

Sean saw Ali's grin, remembering the moment with the driver's tip, and refused to get embarrassed all over again. Giles closed the door after him.

"G'day, mate," said Sean.

Ali was drawn to the bathroom. Sean switched on the TV with the remote control. He always, inexplicably, gave the TV the once-over when they went away. It was some sort of prerequisite. Puffing his chest and slapping his ribs, he wandered to the window to look out at the view.

In the garden below, he saw the little girl. No, *two* little girls. Two identical little girls playing in the sunlight, playing tag in and out of the screw-coned topiary hedges. *Twins. Obviously.* He almost laughed out loud now for being so idiotic.

"En suite!" Ali cried out from the bathroom. "Oh, I do like me en suite! Sean, this is fab! Smellies and everything!"

He turned away from the window, stretched his arms above him and flexed himself, trying to work off the angst of the last half an hour. He went to the bed, upended himself and landed on it on his back like a landed whale. Lying there, he listened to the water running, and his wife humming "Mud, mud, glorious mud…" in the echo-chamber of its tiled ambiance. It was a silly song and it made him smile. She didn't have to do much, when all is said and done, to make him smile. There's a lot to be said for that, he realized. He was a lucky person.

12

"Al? Listen. I'm so sorry."

"Sorry for what?" she said, echoing and splashy from the bathroom. "It's all sorted."

"You come away. The one weekend. It was supposed to be perfect. It was all supposed to be… I don't know…"

He stared at the ceiling, feeling soft and philosophical. Unexpectedly, Ali moved into his field of vision, sitting astride him on the bed. She had undressed and put on a white fluffy hotel bathrobe.

"I'm not complaining," she said. "Do I look as if I'm complaining?"

She untied the robe and lay on him, rolling up his T-shirt, kissing his hairy chest with a mixture of lasciviousness and comic abandon, tweaking his nipples – she knew he hated that – and tickling him relentlessly. Sean was overcome with giggles, play-fighting her off, but really wanting her closer. Closer as closer can get.

"I don't know. We come away for five minutes. You want to control yourself, woman."

"No I don't," she said, her face hovering inches above his.

She got up, pulling him with her by a finger hooked round his trouser-belt, into the bubbling bathroom. Poor old Sean was a lamb to the slaughter.

"Oh yes. En suite!" he cried, succumbing to it all in echoes, in tiling, in the indulgence of Radox. "I do like me en suite!" And their bubbly foreplay was played out to the soundtrack of the end of *Ready Steady Cook* with Ainsley Harriott, which happened to be on TV at the time. Sean entered her to the frantic jiggling of pans and drizzling of sauces as the chefs panicked against the clock. Ali moaning to the rising crescendo of suspenseful theme music. Him massaging her breasts as the sprig of parsley was snipped off. Her going down on him to the choppa-chop rhythm of a knife on basil leaves. Fingers

13

rolling potatoes in butter. Chocolate licked from fingers as he hit the spot. Hopping excitement as Ainsley whipped the audience into the countdown: "*5—4—3—2—1... Stop cooking!*" And the studio audience applauding rapturously.

Some time later, in a dizzy post-sweaty glow, during *The Weakest Link*, Sean finished a wet shave in the bathroom mirror.

"Are they all right? They're not playing you up?" Ali was lying on her tummy on the bed, wearing the towelling bathrobe with the Shewstone House logo on it, her mobile pressed to her ear. She was saying: "You know they've got their Granddad eating out of their hand, the old softie."

Sean came from the bathroom, towel wrapped round his midriff. As she talked, he sat on the bed beside her, still sexually ravenous (or at least peckish) and slowly lifted the bathrobe to reveal her smooth, tightly upholstered behind. She playfully slapped his hand away.

"Well," she said into her phone. "If Hannah has baked beans, Polly has to have baked beans. That's little sisters for you. Pardon?"

Sean kissed each precious buttock. Then he put two paper drinks coasters, one on each cheek of her arse. Ali had serious trouble keeping a straight face and keeping her voice from wavering.

"Sean? Oh yes. He's having a good time too. He's enjoying himself immensely."

While she talked, Sean got up and took the DO NOT DISTURB card from the doorknob and looked at it. He tossed the towel onto the bed, and lowered the DO NOT DISTURB card to hang it on a different kind of knob. At which point Ali really did have trouble keeping a straight face.

They went down to dinner, both feeling a little bit like they were wearing signs saying JUST HAD SEX and SEVERAL TIMES, ACTUALLY. And it made them think how many other couples were there for just that, and might be thinking the same, sheepishly, hunched over their prawn and avocado starters. The barman put two drinks in front of them. "One gin and tonic, one orange juice."

Sean swapped the glasses. His was the orange juice. He worried, fragmentarily, remembering the earlier mix-up with the room booking, and decided to make a joke of it:

"You've never seen me before in your life, correct?"

Ali smiled. The Barman paused, perplexed.

"No, sir."

"Good. Thank you. Cheers."

Sean raised his glass, clinked it against Ali's, and drank.

The dining room was an impressive, candle-lit job with painfully starched tablecloths and silver service, more cutlery and glasses laid out on their one table than they actually owned. Waitresses circulated like monochrome geishas, quietly accommodating, chatty without being intrusive. It occurred to Sean that they were paying over the odds to be made to feel slightly ill at ease. Halfway through the meal he looked over and saw the twin girls sitting at a table with their mother. They were playing tug-of-war with a Sindy doll, and as he watched – while Ali was talking to him about something or other – they began yanking it back and forth quite violently.

Really, *really* violently. The long-necked mother caught his eye and he quickly looked back at Ali.

After eating a bit more he said, "I didn't know Professor Dumbledore was having an affair with Germaine Greer."

Ali looked over her shoulder. Sure enough, there was a couple resembling the hoary old wizard and the hoary old feminist. Tipsy, Ali sniggered. It came out as a bit of a snort, and some of the more stuff-shirted guests looked round in disapproval. She had to bite her lip, cover her mouth to stop a further snort erupting.

"And don't look now but we've got Salvador Dali's brother in."

Ali followed his nod to an extravagantly moustachio'd man, who could be the surrealist painter's clone, and his mousy wife.

She shook her head. "He's probably a hairdresser from Birmingham."

"And she's a librarian. One of those ones in the films where somebody takes off her glasses and says, 'My, but Miss So-and-so, you're beautiful!' No, not for me." Sean broke off to stop the waitress, white blouse, black skirt, black tights, from re-filling his wine glass. But she'd poured some already. "I said 'Not for me.' "

"Sir?"

"I don't drink."

The black-eyed waitress froze. Staring at him. As if flatly disbelieving him at first, then eyes boring into him almost accusingly. Sean stared equally harshly back at her. *What the fuck's going on?*

"I'm very sorry, sir," she said curtly. Too curtly for his liking.

"What do you mean by that?"

She took the soiled glass off onto her silver tray.

"I made a mistake, sir. *Obviously.*" She wasn't just curt, she was sullen now. "Is the table all right for you? I mean, you *did* want the table by the window? Like last week?"

"What do you mean 'last week'?"

The waitress turned on her heel. He grabbed her thin wrist as roughly as he dare.

"What the bloody hell do you mean – *last week*?" Sean had sprung up without thinking and caught the table-edge and knocked over his glass of water. It didn't break, but there was water washing all over his dinner plate and the tablecloth. Ali mopped at the spillage with her napkin and his, embarrassedly aware that all the eyes of the restaurant were on them.

The little waitress's eyes glared at him hard as nail-heads. "You're hurting me. *Sir.*"

Sean let go, and the waitress hurried out of the restaurant.

"Is this you?" Sean turned on his wife. "Is this your idea of a joke or something?"

Ali had stopped laughing and stopped smiling. She was looking right at him with tears of anger and humiliation in her eyes.

"Thank you, Sean."

She grabbed her handbag, got up, took the hotel room key and walked out of the restaurant, leaving her husband alone with the wettened debris, chewing on the anger and frustration dumped on him.

"I'm sorry. I'm sorry!"

"Stop being sorry," she said.

Sean was pacing, taking off his clothes piece by piece by the light of one bedside lamp as Ali finished undressing and threw herself angrily into the double bed and switched off her light. "You'll just have to tell them, that's all."

"Who?"

"The waitress. And that manager."

"Tell them what?"

"Where I was last weekend. Friday, McDonalds with the girls…"

"Saturday, Tesco's and football…"

"Exactly. Sunday, a lie in. And we went to that carvery in Hackney."

"Sean. I *know* where you were."

"Yes, but *they* don't. *They* think I was here!"

"So who *was* here?"

"Christ knows!" said Sean. "Some geezer. Some bloke who looks like me. How do I know?" He ran his hands through his hair, finding his scalp was unnaturally sweaty. He took off his shoes and dropped them with two extravagant thuds.

"Some bloke who looks like you. Who steals your credit card. Who comes here. Why?"

"I have no idea. It was a mix up. She's mistaken. It's two different things. It has to be. Coincidence. It's not impossible. Coincidences happen, don't they?"

Ali sighed, irritated by him and cheesed off. "I don't want to talk about it. I've had enough of it. Can we just not talk about it? Please?"

Sean did as he was asked and shut it. Got in bed, switched off the light on his side. He jiggled round momentarily, trying to get comfortable, then lay stiffly on his back in the hotel darkness, for there is hotel darkness, which is never complete darkness, but has the faint irrepressible glow of the FIRE EXIT sign, and the red wink of the smoke detector light.

He sighed a sigh designed for his wife to hear. He thought it was a bit too obvious when he heard it himself. He didn't like to be that obvious, personally. It was hotel warm, an artificial warmth you only get in hotels and coffins, as artificial as the Shake-n-Vac carpet cleaner that was meant to be fragrant but, he found, really clawed at the back of your throat. It made him want to gag, often. There wasn't any fragrance any more. And he couldn't believe that the figure in bed next to him was the one he had enjoyed tremendous sex with only a few hours previously. Now, a small part of him cried out to touch her skin, but a larger part of him wanted to scream at her.

A strong wind was cultivating outside, and after some time in the gloom, Sean was aware of the fingertip tapping of raindrops hitting the glass of the window on the other side of the heavy Laura Ashley curtains.

Outside, the hotel was floodlit – artificial, again – an island in the storm. A vandal breeze buffeted patio canopies and had overturned several identical garden chairs. Trees shuddered. A swing swung. The topiaries – round, conical, spirals – cast deep shadows on the greens. The light over the main entrance came on, remained on for a few seconds, then went off, the same thing happening repeatedly, triggered by the gale which seemed now to be acting like a naughty schoolboy knocking someone's front door and then running off.

Still life. The digital alarm clock – hotel, artificial – read: 2.15 AM. Beside it sat Sean's watch, ticking, a thick airport novel, and Sean's open wallet, open at the reject passport photo of Ali he always kept there. Not far from this was the enormous, fluffy pillow on which Sean's head rested, or tried to, unsuccessfully. He was used to cheap, flat pillows, and these monstrosities were sprayed with something that unsettled him. Unsettled his sinuses. Alarmed him, somewhat, somehow. *Fragrant.* Finally he shifted, from lying on his front to lying on his back. But even then he was even less comfortable than before, and after the third contortion, less comfortable than that. How many times would he change position before becoming a total twisted bloody jelly? *Shit-balls.* In the stillness of the shadowy room, he tossed and turned, unable to achieve anything approximating sleep.

He buried his face in the fluff-cloud. But soon his cheek burned like fever and he lay on his back – he never slept on his back – just to get breath. He lay in perspiration. *Bloody hotel heating.* But he knew if he got up to wash, he'd revive himself and would be awake for hours. He lay in his sweat and hoped to dream. But he didn't dream, at least he thought he didn't.

It was impossible to cut out all the manifold and sometimes dubious sounds of the hotel. He followed footsteps as some prat had room service delivered. He wanted to cheer when the footsteps finally faded away. Then…

In the next room. Footsteps. A door opening and closing. Footsteps. A thump. Bedsprings. Murmurings. Laughter. A man and a woman. A door banging hard and…

Sean's eyes flashed open.

Awake.

He turned on his side, silently. *Trying* to listen now, he wasn't sure why, but it was impossible *not* to listen. There was no doubt about the sound he heard. He was being treated to the sounds of someone's lovemaking gently filtered through the wall. He realised he was unable to move, and, very soon, unable to breathe, as the sounds became more passionate, the bed-head knocking the wall more rhythmic, the ghastly springs squealing like a mouse skipping round the innards of a church-organ, the woman's voice pantingly bereft, grasping, bucking, lurching – did he think *lurching?* – then snarling louder and louder…

"No, no, no, uh, uh, uh, uh, uh, uhh, uhhhh…"

Eyes trying to stay clamped shut, Sean reached out for the bedside phone and pressed "0" for Reception. He could hear the phone ringing at the other end of the line as, in his other ear, he heard the woman in the next room come to orgasm. Then the room went quiet.

Nobody was answering the burr-burr of the phone, so in the end he hung up. Let out a long breath. Turned over, restless, impatient. Tired beyond tiredness. *Then…* After a few beats he heard voices, almost under the radar, but clear as a bell.

"Did you enjoy that?" A woman.

"Yes. Thank you very much." The man.

A pause.

The woman chuckled.

"What?" said the man. "What's so funny?"

" 'Thank you very much.' Like your Mum told you to say it."

The woman laughed again.

The man laughed too.

Then it went quiet.

Until the man said: "What's so funny about my Mum telling me to say it?"

Pause.

"Nothing. Don't look at me like that. *Nothing*'s funny, all right?"

SLAP.

Sean felt like he was slapped himself. Then he heard another *SLAP* – then silence. He wasn't sure if he had imagined it. Maybe it was the sound of something else. Maybe he was mistaken. Maybe he wasn't quite as awake as he thought. He cranked up his head at an angle from the pillow.

There was silence in the next room. He was afraid to breathe. Then…

"No, if it's funny, it's funny," said the man's voice, not raised at all. "If it's funny, why aren't you *laughing*? Eh?"

Sean sat up in bed, silently, his bare feet touching the floor.

Now the woman wasn't laughing. She was sobbing. She was weeping.

"You're hurting me. You're hurting me!"

He stood up and pulled on his jeans rapidly. He came out into the corridor, barefoot. At the end of the corridor he could see a pair of lift doors with a sign reading: OUT OF ORDER. He hadn't noticed the sign before. It must have been put there recently. He was in Room 23 and the room next to him was Room 24. That's what it said on the door, the door he was now staring at. It was dead silent in there. He nervously backed away from it, the door, staring at it a few seconds more before going downstairs without shoes on.

The on/off light from outside cast an erratic glow. *On.* He came down the history-riddled, Henry VIII stairs and padded to the desk. *Photos?* It wasn't manned, but the screen of the VDU was still on, with some super-helix screen-saver spinning round on it hypnotically. *Off.* He walked around the hall area, peering into the bar, then into the lounge. Both looked like the Mary Celeste. *On.* He heard some swing doors open and some footsteps.

The assistant manager had a love bite on his neck which Sean didn't seem to remember seeing before. *Off.*

"Ah, Mr Merritt, are you happy with your new room?"

Sean looked at him open-mouthed. He blinked like a fish.

"What are you talking about?"

The assistant manager seemed just as baffled as he was.

"Er... The room I just took you to? You rang about ten minutes ago to complain about the noise from the neighbours."

Sean blinked again. "No I didn't."

The assistant manager laughed nervously, as if Sean was trying to catch him out. But he could see that Sean was deadly serious. In fact the young man didn't enjoy seeing slow, confused horror creep over a customer's face. He did what he was told, and accompanied Sean quickly back upstairs, with the key to Room 24.

"Here. This is it. Open it," said Sean when they got there, realising that he was still bathed in his layer of hotel-bed sweat.

"But, sir..."

"Open it, for God's sake."

The assistant manager turned his skeleton key in the lock. The door opened an inch. The room was dark within. Sean could hear the sound of a woman's muffled groaning, her dry lips parting, a sound as if frightened, hurt.

The assistant manager stepped trepidatiously into the gloom and Sean reached past him in a blur to turn on the light. The woman's breath caught in her throat as light flooded the room. Sean rushed in. His heart caught in his mouth with shock. He couldn't get his head round what he saw. He reined himself in from shock to puzzlement, as a self-preservation mechanism, but the thudding in his chest told him otherwise.

He was looking at the mirror of his own room. Room 23. This room was identical, he could see that, but the layout was exactly reversed. But that isn't what made him feel someone was standing on his thorax in hob-nail boots. What did that was the fact that Ali, his wife, was sitting up in bed, groggily blinking awake.

"What is it?" she asked, more than half asleep, deciphering the blurry, uncertain figure at the door. "Sean? What's happening?"

Stunned for a moment, frozen and feeling his sweat go unaccountably icy too, Sean switched the light off again. He went to the bed, a shadow now, and leaned over and kissed her and tucked her in.

"I'm sorry, love. Go to sleep," he whispered.

Seconds later he was back out in the corridor where the assistant manager was standing. Hardly looking at him, Sean went straight to the door to Room 23. *His* room. He pointed at it accusingly.

"Open it. *Open* it."

Again, the assistant manager did as he was told, again, he didn't have much choice. His keys rattled. The rain lashed at numerous panes of glass. Sean started to take some kind of control of his breathing and was momentarily happy when he had. The assistant manager prodded the door inwards and stepped back. Sean stepped inside.

He switched on the light.

And found Room 23 – what exactly had he been expecting? – totally pristine. Untouched. Empty. Uninhabited. Spotless. As if the housemaids had just walked out. Bottled water untouched. Bed and pillows unwrinkled and unruffled, and most definitely un-copulated in. What the hell was going on?

"I must be going mad."

He reversed out into the corridor. The assistant manager closed the door to Room 23 and locked it with his jangling ring of keys. Sean looked at him, trying to find some kind of apology, but couldn't. The assistant manager smiled. What the hell he smiled for, Sean had absolutely no bloody idea.

With the young man's eyes still on him, Sean went sheepishly back to his room – his new room, the one with number 24 on the door. He felt deeply uncomfortable touching the handle – it felt slimy and hot – but turned it and pressed it shut after him. He lay in the hotel dark and waited for sleep to come, wondering if the assistant manager was still out there in the corridor, monkey-suited and with the love bite on his neck, staring at the door of the room, smiling, because he hadn't heard his footsteps walk away.

There's nothing like the sound of birds singing brightly to dissipate the blues of bad dreams. Sean drifted up into consciousness with an innate yearning to be an ornithologist, to identify his little feathered friends, to hold them in his hand and kiss them on the little beaks. He sensed a golden glow of morning on the far side of his eyelids. It was only with the waking that he realised how much he had been desperate, really *desperate* to get to sleep, and that (or was it the plush bouncy bed, wide as a kingdom?) gave him a feeling of innate and all-consuming bliss.

The radio alarm had clicked on with an easy listening version of "The Girl from Ipenama". (Was there any other version?) Images of swishing hips in a grass skirt flitted across his mind's eye, stupidly. His face was buried in his pillow, smiling more broadly to every swish. He swallowed and gulped air before lying on his back in the yellow spotlight that fell across the duvet and forced his lids to open.

Under the Disneyesque birdsong he could hear the bathroom taps gushing indulgently. He saw that the bed next to him was a rumpled, empty space with the cover tossed back and a dent in the pillow. A wife-shaped dent. He smelled her nice smell of last night's lipstick and night-care skin milk, the one he'd bought for her birthday, and the image of her rubbing it into her legs last thing before bed added to the bliss.

"That's it," he said loud enough to be heard in the en suite. "No more coffee for me. Strictly decaf or nothing!" He put on his watch, noticing the strap was beginning to fray at the hole. He made a mental note to buy a new one when they got home next week. "Ali? Hey…" He downloaded the dream from his memory, more in curiosity, now, than alarm. "Did they give us Room 23 or Room 24 last night?"

He wanted to know but there was no answer.

He sat up, back creaking a little. He wasn't used to the level of comfort of last night, there had to be a price to pay, naturally. The way of the world. He felt the soles of his feet touch the chill of the carpet.

"Ali?"

Still no answer.

He stood up and walked over, only accidentally aware of the daylight and the bright emerald green of the lawns outside the window, and entered the bathroom.

In the parallel mirrors, hotel-sharp and unforgiving, he saw that he was reflected back on himself into perpetuity, like some childish fairground-ride kind of thing and it twanged him to infanthood and back like an elastic band. He saw himself older and more world-worn than he liked to think, but then he avoided mirrors at the best of times. He instinctively turned away from them and looked at Ali, ready to make some remark about that, but all he saw was an empty Victorian repro claw-foot bath, with scalding-

26

hot water spiraling down the plughole. And Ali? Where was Ali? Where was his wife?

She laughed. Ali laughed. He heard her laughter. It was hers. No question. It twanged him back to a weekend in Brighton on a penis-shrinkingly cold winter's day, it yanked him sideways to kissing her breast and tickling each other in bed, it slapped his face to walking down the aisle, not that there was an aisle but there was a registry office and a best man dressed as a matador.

It was Ali's laughter and it was coming from outside.

He turned from his many reflections and rushed, stumbling against unfamiliar furniture to the window, yanking back the heavy drapes, clawing back the multiple layers of net, flattening his hands and his face to the glass, sunlight direct in his eyes, looking down and seeing below him the driveway, and then he could see her, there.

Ali in a raincoat and red high heels, with a man in a black coat beside her. Sean couldn't see his face, he could only see him from the back. She was in profile now, laughing again. Sean wanted to cry out her name but he knew he wouldn't be heard. He felt trapped like an animal in a cage. Their footsteps were silent on the chippings. They were walking now, starting up the long drive, at a leisurely pace. Arm in arm. Like lovers.

And Sean stared, because he could no nothing much more than stare, at first. Because when the man in the black overcoat looked back over his shoulder and then up, up at Sean as if knowing he was there looking down at them, then gave him a knowing little wink as he put his arm around Ali's shoulder, Sean saw with peculiar clarity that his wife was leaving the hotel on the arm of himself. *Himself, grinning.*

He fought with the window latch that sprang into sharp focus now, but it was locked with a key. He launched back to the bed, grabbing his jeans and pulling them on, not bothering with underpants or socks.

A sedate octogenarian couple were taking one step at a time up the stairs as this maniac came crashing like a stuntman down at them, through them, blinded by the T-shirt he was pulling over his head, revolving disorientatedly in the reception area now, laces undone.

Sean ran out of the main doors into a sunlight so bright he thought his cornea blasted. It stopped him dead. His lungs were telling him he'd run several marathons but in fact it was panic constricting his chest like several tightening loops of metal.

The driveway stretched out ahead of him, a quarter of a mile across the green lawns and immaculate garden to the wrought iron gates. And there wasn't a soul in sight.

He turned, looked round three hundred and sixty degrees. Nothing. Nobody. Just the doddery old gardener examining a rose bush, tending it lovingly with a dribble from a long-spouted watering can.

"There was a man and a woman. Where did they go? Did you see where they went?"

"Morning sir. Sorry?"

"A man and woman. Just now. Did you see them?"

"Man?"

"And a woman. Yes. Here, just now."

The gardener just stared at him, adopting a frowning, thoughtful blankness. Sean rushed back inside.

He looked round at the various hotel guests milling towards breakfast. Giles, the Australian helper, stood to one side. He had zoomed past him on the way out.

"Giles. Have you seen my wife? Did you see my wife going past you in the last five minutes?"

"No. Have you tried the breakfast room, sir?"

Sean ran into the breakfast room. Did a quick circuit. Dashed out again.

"Can I help you, sir?" said the assistant manager.

Sean ignored him and ran straight back outside. Without pausing he headed up the driveway, breaking into a run, legs pumping like a sprinter now. He hadn't run like that in years. He couldn't remember when he'd last run like that. The adrenaline was flowing and he had to use it or it would burn up, burn him up. Somehow, instinctively he knew that, or felt it. He knew he had to run.

He'd almost reached the gates when the mini-bus turned into the driveway and slammed on its brakes. He slapped his hands gecko-like on the wide windscreen. The mini-bus juddered to a halt. A few shrieks were uttered and as Sean got his breath back he saw passengers beyond the driver, all dressed up in wedding togs, tuxedos and bridesmaid dresses.

"Have you seen my wife?" Sean asked the driver. "You've come on the road from the station? There's only one road, right?"

"Yes, sir."

"Did you see her? With a man."

"No, sir."

"Are you sure?"

"There's no footpath, sir. And I'd notice somebody walking along the road." The driver addressed his passengers. "Anybody see anyone?" There was only a chorus of various phrases in the negative, a lot of shaking of heads, and a bullet-headed guy called Sean a tosser. The guy had the letters spelling L-O-V-E on his fingers. Sean could see it as he tapped the driver's shoulder to get a move on.

S ean sat in the manager's office, head in hands, trying to keep his cool but wanting to go nuts and trash the place with its stupid Habitat desk light and stupid IN and OUT trays, year planner and idiotic office toys. Opposite him sat a WPC in uniform. She was youngish, far too young for Sean's liking. She should be swatting for her GCSEs as far as he was concerned. She was pretty, with straw-like hair and a rural ruddiness to her cheeks. But she had a masculine jaw-line and was nobody's fool. He could see her breaking someone's arm with a truncheon at a peace demonstration, no problem.

"You don't think it's likely your wife might have wandered off on her own?" said the WPC, whose name Sean had already forgotten.

"Look. I saw her from the window. With this man."

"So you think they may have gone off together, is that what you mean?"

"Yes. What else would I mean? Yes."

"So have you seen this man before? Do you know him?"

Sean thought for a moment. His head sank into his hands again and he rubbed his forehead vigorously as if trying to remove an indelible stain. What could he possibly say? That the man who made off with his wife looked identical to him?

"No," he said. "I don't... know him."

"Can you give me a description of him?"

"No. I only saw the back of his head. Look, why don't you put out an APB or whatever the hell it is you people do and just *find* her? Please!"

"Did you try her mobile?"

"Do I look like an idiot?" He pulled it out of his pocket, thrust it out at her. "It was beside the bed upstairs, where she left it."

"Have you checked it for any unusual incoming calls?"

"Yes. There aren't any. Check if you like, if that's what you want to do."

"No, sir," she said. "I believe you."

You – hold on, did you just say what I think you said?

Before he could say anything the WPC looked at her watch. "She's been gone for, what? Eight o'clock-ish? So say, three hours? So she's not exactly *missing*, exactly?"

"So what *is* she, then? *Mislaid* or something? She'll turn up, is that what you're saying? Like a coin down the back of the bloody…"

"You seem unduly anxious, sir."

"I'm not *unduly* anxious. I just…"

"I understand you and your wife had words last night in the restaurant."

"Words?" Then he remembered. No point denying it. He wasn't going to lie to her. "OK, words. Yes. So?"

"With respect, sir… you see, I'm a woman." *Really?* "I know what women are like, how they think, and…"

"Yeah," said Sean. "And I'm her husband. I know what my wife is like, and what she would or wouldn't do, thank you very much."

"It's just that, if I had a barney with my husband, I don't know, I might just high-tail it for a while, leave the old bugger to stew for a bit." It was the first time she betrayed her country accent.

Sean let out a sigh and shook his head, making it plain he disagreed with the local yokel's particular assessment. Not that he had anything spectacular to replace it with.

"And what about the man?" he said.

She looked at him inscrutably.

"What exactly did you see, Mr Merritt? Someone leaving the hotel? A passing joke, perhaps, between two people? Your wife was laughing, you said. Abducted people don't laugh, do they? People in danger don't laugh."

Sean said nothing at that point.

He sat simmering and examined his thumbs.

The WPC stood up, pocketed her notebook, and put on her gloves.

"My money, she'll show up by lunchtime. You can make up. Kiss kiss."

Sean glowered at her.

She put on her peaked cap, aware maybe that she'd stepped over the line into facetiousness, and softened. "I seriously don't think there's any need to panic, sir. Not at this early stage. This isn't the seething metropolis out here. The nearest thing we have to a crime wave here is a stolen bike." Sean didn't smile, if a smile was expected of him, tough. "You stay put here at the hotel. If she hasn't been in touch in a couple of hours, we'll start making enquiries. OK?" She carefully put her chair under the desk in the position she'd found it. Her eyes fell upon Sean again and she said quietly: "Is there anything else you want to tell me?"

Sean was thinking: *Yes. Yes, the voices in the next room, the slaps, the weeping, the room next door, the Visa card, the mistaken identity with the waitress, the assistant manager's love bite… God, Christ.*

But what he said was:

"No. Nothing. I appreciate your concern, officer."

He didn't quite know if the WPC detected his sarcasm before she left.

There was nothing he could think of doing except he knew Ali'd promised to phone the girls first thing in the morning at her grandparents' to check they were OK, and it wasn't first thing anymore. He returned to his room and stood by the window, looking out, as he made a call on his mobile.

"No. Daddy just wanted to talk to you, darling." As he stared down at the driveway he was afraid even to blink in case he missed something. What could he miss? He'd missed the most important thing already. Ali was gone. His eyes had begun to prickle, he blinked them and the dryness was medicated by a glaze of tears. He listened to his daughter's voice. "No, darling. Mummy – Mummy's not here just now. Mummy'll talk to you later, OK? Yes, promise."

He felt desperately isolated in the big room. A maid moved around, robotically making the bed, straightening the side where Ali had slept, freshly tight, tucking it in, and puffing the dent from the pillow as if she'd never been there. It made Sean shudder and he wanted the maid to leave so that he could weep in peace. Not that peace was anything to do with it.

Later he sat on a cold stone bench by a flower bush in the hotel grounds. The prettiness of the garden did nothing to lift his feeling of being out of control. Not him, the world was out of control. He was twitchy as hell. He felt shell-shocked. Worse than shell-shocked – this was something he felt he alone was suffering, something inexplicable to others, some punishment targeted upon him alone. And even as he thought it, he knew it made no sense: none of it made sense, at all. He had ants in his pants. He got up and crossed the drive, looking up the length of it to the far-off wrought-iron gates, willing Ali to reappear by magic since she had disappeared in the same fashion. It didn't happen. The ancient gardener was pruning. The twins, the two little girls he saw the day before, were playing croquet, Alice-like, and their laughter was horribly delightful. He was compelled to shut it out.

Feeling numb and devoid of hope, Sean turned and looked over his shoulder up at the hotel.

He realised with a chill that he was standing, looking up at the window of his room, in the exact same spot where his double had been standing. It made him feel sick.

He turned away, catching sight through the ground floor bay window of a waitress in the restaurant. He recognised her straight away as the waitress they'd had the night before.

She was clearing the last debris of lunch and setting the linen, cutlery and glasses for dinner that evening when he came through and approached her. She was unaware of him entering the room until he was quite close, and when she did see him she jumped with a little start of alarm. The cutlery tinkled. Sean didn't move. She didn't say anything and abruptly returned to her work.

"Do I know you?" asked Sean, trying not to sound confrontational. He didn't want to be confrontational. He just wanted to know the truth.

She looked at him with lazy disdain. "After last weekend?"

"What happened last weekend?"

She laughed, like the word *pathetic* was on her lips ready to come out.

"I wasn't here last weekend," said Sean, as non-aggressively as he could manage. "Do you think I'm somebody else, or what exactly?"

"I know who you are," said the waitress confidently. "Does she?"

"Look – I don't know what you're talking about, but…"

"Of course not." She tweaked a red wine glass. "I get it."

"Get *what*?"

"I just didn't have you down as a married man. You were about the most *un*-married man I've ever met."

"So you *have* met me? Someone who looks like me?"

She stared at him hard. Tired of it now, pissed off with him. "Oh, get lost." She tried to walk past him, ending the conversation, but he side-stepped and blocked her.

"No, please. Tell me."

She curled her lip, eyes burning. "This Mr Nice Guy act might work on her indoors, but don't try it on me, all right?"

"Act? What *act*? Wait a minute."

She picked up a full tray and crossed the room to the double swing doors to the kitchen.

"Help me," said Sean, following her. "Tell me about this man who looks like me. You know about him. Who is he? What's his name?" He was close behind, close enough to touch, not wanting to let her get away. She turned and looked him in the eyes and he saw toughness, and bravery, and hurt, and little glinting slivers of pain, and little sharp thorns of love.

"His name's Sean Merritt. He said he'd be with me. This weekend. Without fail. He promised. Remember?" She opened the swing door with her behind. He followed.

"Look. I've never been to this place before in my life. I swear. You've got to believe me."

"Oh sure," she said. "Believe you?"

"I'm not who you think I am."

She almost swore, but there were other kitchen staff around, maybe her boss, and he was a customer after all. "Is this your idea of 'patching things up'? Shoving your wife in my face?"

"What did he do? *Tell* me."

"Who?"

"The man who looks like me."

The waitress almost laughed. "You're sick." She punched the controls of a dishwashing machine. It

35

rumbled into its wash cycle. She pressed her hands on top of it, as if afraid what she might do with them otherwise.

"He's taken my wife. For God's sake, help me. Please."

Something in Sean's voice made her turn and look at him, properly now. It was the face of a man scared and desperate. And whatever she felt afraid of or disgusted by, he could tell, she didn't see there anymore. She saw, to her distress and not a little confusion, someone as afraid and hurt and desperate as she was. And he saw his little feathered friends and thought how easy they were to break in your hand, and how beautiful they were up close, if you could get close without them flying away.

The swing doors banged opened and the chef came in, belly first and ego close behind. He proceeded to give his sous chef a bollocking. Sean looked down and saw that his own hand was gripping the girl's spindly arm. Chef turned and looked at him. Sean let go and held up his palms apologetically and backed away, heading out of chef's realm before it was him who got a roasting. He paused at the double doors to look back at the young waitress.

"Help me," he said.

She watched him go and tried hard not to think about his words, or the look on his face.

Sean sat down at the bar. A cloth moved back and forth polishing it.

"The usual, sir?"

Sean looked up at him. It was a different barman from the night before, smiling like he had too many teeth in his head. Sean said nothing and felt gnawingly sick again. The barman measured a double Jameson's from an optic on the wall and placed it in front of him. Sean stared down at it.

"What happened to the other barman?"

"Oh, Ian from The Grapes? Last night? He was filling in for me. It was my night off."

Nauseous, Sean got up and left the bar, and the barman, and the whiskey, intact. He passed the reception desk on his way upstairs, but the bank-advert-looking girl hailed him over with a raised, beckoning finger.

"Ah, Mr Merritt? Excuse me. I think you have a message…"

Sean back-tracked down the stairs and walked over.

"Is it from the policewoman? Has she got any news?"

The girl gave him an envelope from a pigeon-hole behind her.

"I don't know, sir. I just saw it in the box for your room. Room 24."

Sean looked at the envelope, examined it front and back, then walked out onto the terrace. He sat himself at a patio table. Not far away a bride and groom were posing for being photographed against the lush flower beds and fake Grecian statues. She had flowers in her hair. He had shiny gel on his.

Sean opened the envelope and found, firstly, one of the Shewstone House DO NOT DISTURB cards, the ones you hang on the outside door handle of your room. Secondly, a photograph. The passport photograph of Ali he always carried in his wallet.

The bride and groom's chuckling wafted towards him but he felt ice cold in spite of the heat. He looked at the back of the envelope and his heart quickened horribly as he saw a thumb print in red ink… is it red ink? Or is it –

He walked across the terrace. He stuck his thumb in the soil of a potted plant. Extracting it, he made a grubby imprint beside the red one. He raised it up in front of his eyes, the sun on his back, squinting, focusing. Trying to convince himself and his eyes that the two thumbprints were not – could not be – identical.

More guffaws and high jinks from the photography group made him look up. He hastily put the passport photo and the NO NOT DISTURB card back in the envelope, and the envelope in his inside jacket pocket. He tugged his cuffs and coughed into his hand and walked back inside.

He went up to his room. To Room 24. He went straight to the bedside table, and saw the same still life of alarm clock, airport novel, and his open wallet, still full of money, twenties, tens, but with a space where the passport photograph of Ali used to be.

In the en suite he rinsed water over his face, rubbing it forcefully into his tired eyes and slicking it back through his hair. He wanted to wake up. He wanted to wake up *from this*. He saw the dirty black soil-mark on his thumb and rubbed it off, grinding it into the palm of his other hand until it was gone.

When he turned off the sink taps he began to hear a faint but distinct noise – a tap, tap, tap…

It stopped for a moment and he listening. Then, there it was again.

Tap, tap, tap…

He stepped out into the bedroom and looked round, trying to detect where it was coming from. It was probably nothing. His mind doing the works on everything since the morning. Was it any wonder? He was about to turn on the radio to kill the silence when, there it was again.

Tap, tap, tap…

For all the world like a witch's crooked finger on a window pane. Yes, that was exactly where it was coming from. The window.

He turned. Beyond the glass something was dangling on a string, like a ghastly pendulum, some object swinging and knocking against the glass repetitively. A plastic doll's face, Barbie-blonde hair hanging, blue eyes open, quickly whipped out of sight – *gone*.

Sean opened the bottom sash and leaned out. He twisted his head, looking up.

Directly above him, a window was open and the twin girls he'd seen before were leaning out. They hauled up their Sindy doll, which they had been dangling on a piece of string tied to her ankles, upside down, next to his window. Now the two cheekily grinning faces disappeared quickly inside, Sindy disappearing with them, blonde hair, blue eyes – gone.

Leaving Sean to duck back inside, close the window as the window higher up also closed, and pull the curtains shut. He heard the children's laughter in the room above, getting louder and louder in his head. He stared at the ceiling, picturing the twins tossing the doll one to the other, laughing at him, laughing endlessly at the joke.

Darkness didn't exactly fall. Light passed from the sky according to the laws of nature, yes, but Shewstone House was still lit by the floodlights embedded in the grounds, disguised by bushes and bedding plants, bathing its Bath-stone glory in a honeycomb hue. Cracks of inner light shone from a few windows as guests spruced themselves up, or dressed, or watered, or fondled, or frolicked. Already the soundtrack of the evening was being provided by the wedding reception underway in the function room, its own notable light show pulsating in all directions, frightening off prowling vixens and other scavengers. Village People and Cockney Rebel vied with the night. There were more cars in the car park and wedding revellers staggered round on the chippings outside the hotel, puffing fags or guzzling beer or spirits with loosened collars, dangling ties, and suspect footwork. If they couldn't stagger, they sure as hell couldn't dance, however much Frankie Goes to Hollywood implored them to.

In Room 24, Sean lay on the bed, staring at the ceiling, fully dressed. He was utterly exhausted but knew he would not be able to sleep, or even shut his eyes. The music of the wedding disco was muffled, turning to Ibiza dance music now, an insistent beat which was too much like the hammering he felt inside his skull to think of it as a welcome distraction. It just added to the torture. That and the knowledge there were people down there – married couples down there – enjoying themselves as if nothing had happened. What *had* happened, exactly? A gentle knock on the door broke his thought pattern, and he was grateful to it.

"Yes?"

"Room service," said a voice.

Puzzled, he crossed the room and opened the door. The skinny little waitress he had spoken to in the restaurant stood there. She looked down, resolutely avoiding his eyes, pushing a trolley on which sat a silver salver, napkin in a ring, knife, fork, spoon, glass. As she moved round the bed and started to lay the starched white cloth on the side-table, as was expected of her, it was obvious she was uncomfortable seeing him, didn't want to be there, and it made Sean uncomfortable too.

"I didn't order anything," he said.

She stopped. She said nothing, still didn't look at him. She looked pained and continued laying the table as if he hadn't spoken, or wasn't even there. When she'd finished she held out a slip of paper stiffly, the tongue of a till roll.

"Would you sign this please, sir?"

"No. Talk to me. Please."

She stiffened, aware of the empty bed. "Where is she?"

"She's gone. I told you. He took her." The waitress was already heading to the door. "Please. Don't go."

She stopped halfway and turned back.

"Something's happened to you," she said. "You're not the same."

"I'm *not* the same. I'm trying to tell you. The person you think I am is somebody else. I know it sounds…"

"Two people don't look that alike. Not unless they're twins. And you said you were an only child."

"When?" The penny dropped. "He told you that? He knows that about me? What else does he know?"

She didn't answer.

Sean decided not to push her. He didn't want to hurt her, verbally or otherwise. She looked frightened enough as it was. Suddenly he felt like a puppet whose strings were cut and he had to sit down before he fell down. It had built up and built up, this weight, and suddenly it was too much. His head was swimming and he sat down on the bed corner, gazing into space, lost and scared beyond belief. Ignoring the girl now.

She became even more uncomfortable and adjusted her black, tight, waitress skirt. "They'll be wanting me downstairs."

"Stay. Please."

He didn't dare look up at her. Then he felt the weight of her sitting on the other corner of the bed, not close to him but close enough. He still felt she didn't want to be there and he wondered why she was.

"He has my wife. I have to know about him. I have to find out what happened." Then he asked her face directly. "What happened last weekend?"

41

"Fuck the new legislation. Have you got a cigarette?"

"I don't smoke."

She tensed. "He does. Silk Cut. Keeps the lighter tucked in the packet."

Sean looked blank. She could see he knew nothing about it. Unless he was a very, very good actor.

"Is this amnesia or something? Have you had a bang on the head?"

"I don't know what it is. All I know is my wife is missing and I saw her with him. With *me*."

She parted her lips, really wanting that cigarette now. "You said you'd come back and see me. You said you'd be here. You promised it would be good this time." Her throat tightened a tiny bit. "I believed you."

Sean realised they were talking in whispers, like in church.

"What did he say to you?"

She shrugged. "He was alone. Travelling between tournaments. Table all to himself…"

"Tournaments?"

She nodded. "Snooker. You're a snooker player. Professional. Champion. On the telly, you say. Suit worth a bit. More than a bit. Clean hair…" Her eyes roamed over Sean, from his forehead to the tips of his toes. "He doesn't sit like that. He sits like he owns the place. Brandy. A few. Monte Cristo cigars on the terrace. Wants me to have a drink with him… Have a *chat*…"

He noticed she said *chat* like it was an ugly, obscene word. He stood up and took the wine bottle from the room service trolley. He twisted the corkscrew into it and poured one glass and handed it to her. Her hands had been pressed flat to the bedcover till that moment.

"Restaurant's empty now," she continued as she took it. "No harm in that. Then the brandy bottle's on the table. I say, 'No thanks.' He says, 'Come on. Nightcap.' The

42

bar's about to shut. He says, 'I'm off to my room, then, Monica. Catch up on my beauty sleep.' He puts the brandy bottle on my tray and he looks at me in the eyes and says, 'Room Service?' Just like that." She drank some wine, getting rid of a lump in her throat. Lowered her chin as she swallowed. "And he goes upstairs."

Sean felt his palms prickling. He felt he had to say something but he didn't want to. It was already more than he wanted to hear, but he had to hear more. Much more.

"Did you fancy him?"

"He's a type. I know I'm nothing to him. But he wants me. I feel like being wanted, for a change."

"I'm sorry."

"Why?"

"You sound like you've been hurt."

Monica smiled, trying to make it a bitter one but just making it clearer he was right. "You can't be sorry for everyone that's been hurt." She wasn't uncomfortable with him anymore, he thought, but she didn't like looking into his eyes. *His* eyes. "This is cold." She stood up and took the silver dome lid from the room service meal. A strong smell erupted, catching Sean unawares. "Tiger prawns in garlic sauce."

"I hate prawns," said Sean. "I hate garlic." Ali always got irritated with him saying that, always castigated him for not trying things that were exotic, in spite of his likes and dislikes. She said his prejudices were brainwashing by his mother and said his mother wasn't there anymore. *I hate garlic.* That kind of statement was no longer banal. Under the present circumstances it was deeply horrifying. Monica stared down at the food in front of her, her back to him. Her tiny waist. Bony shoulders. "What does he like? What does he hate?" He wanted to know something. Anything. "Monica…?"

As he watched, she unbuttoned her sleeve and rolled it up to her elbow. Her head tilted to one side, accidentally in an attitude of coyness, and he didn't like that. Gradually revealed was a nasty bruise, purple and livid, running right up the inside softness of her arm. Sean was shocked enough by that. His scrotum constricted and a spasm ran though him. Then she turned to face him and slowly unbuttoned the neck of her blouse. He saw a vivid love bite between one breast and her collar bone. The spasm in Sean's body became a horrid ache, and though it was nothing to do with him – *was* it to do with him? – he was upset and felt somehow responsible. Yes, responsible. From the disco down below pounded "I'm Too Sexy for My Shirt", flaunting, foppish, ridiculous, agonising.

"That's not all," said Monica.

She turned her back and lifted up the hair that covered the back of her neck. Sean stood up and moved closer. He saw several brown scars smaller than five pence pieces, he took them at first to be moles, but they were too alike in shape and density, and almost gagged as he realized they were cigarette burns. She didn't turn to look at him as she spoke.

"He did it from behind. I didn't want to. He knew that. He knew I couldn't scream. If anybody knew I was in the room… I realised that was why he asked me in the first place. It was his plan." She held the edge of the metal trolley. He couldn't see her face but heard her sniff back tears.

"My God," he said. "I'm sorry, I'm so…"

He felt he should do something, not to compensate but as a natural human response. He wasn't sure it was right but he trusted his instinct. He touched the base of her neck with trembling fingers. She turned, unmistakable tears welling up in her eyes now. Tears of anger.

44

"Have I turned you on, then? Have I?"

Sean was shocked. "No. God, no."

The tears sparkled as she whipped her face away.

"You said you loved me. You said you were sorry. You said you'd explain. This weekend you'd come back to the hotel. You'd make it up to me."

"And he *has* come back."

"Make it up to me. What does that mean? 'Make it up to me?' "

"But this time it's not you," said Sean. "He's not interested in you. It's Ali. It's Ali he wants to hurt this time. Oh God. Oh Jesus Christ…"

Sean paced up and down like a bear in a cage. In a luxurious cage. And as she looked at him and saw the absolute fear and horror and helplessness in his face, in his walk, in his shape, in his soul, she knew she couldn't accuse him any more.

"You love her, don't you?"

He said, "More than anything."

For several seconds neither of them moved. The disco beat was getting to him again. He sat on the bed with his back to her, elbows cemented to his knees, hands cemented to his cheeks. He did not know what more to do. He had to be alone. Please, alone. He had to think about Ali. He had to think about *him*. He thought Monica would leave the room then, but she didn't. She walked around to him and turned his face to hers and kissed him on the lips. He didn't want it, but he did.

"You're not like him," she said, backing away.

"Thank you."

She gathered the stuff on the trolley, including the bottle and glass of wine, and wheeled it out into the corridor. Sean closed the door after her and leaned the front of his head against it when she'd gone. Hot

Chocolate sung that they believed in miracles. Sean didn't know what he believed any more.

The moronic beat returned, DJ in full swing. After a while Sean went to the bathroom and washed his face again, and as he dried off with the towel, dripping, he looked at himself in the mirror. At his reflection, at his left cheek then his right. Is that what he looks like, this monster, this madman? Him? He heard footsteps outside his room and he was sure he heard Ali's voice saying "Not like that, like this!"

He ran to the door and flung it open and poked his head out into the corridor, darting a glance right and left.

The corridor was empty. Empty except for the figure of the mother with one of her twins, who was dressed in daffodil-yellow as a bridesmaid. Mum, too, was done up as if for the wedding in a calf-length frock. She was bent over her daughter like a dentist, half obscuring the child's face. The child was making guttural noises, standing stiffly with its mouth wide while the mother delved deep into her mouth with two fingers. A gurgling, choking noise assaulted Sean's ears. Aware of being watched, the mother stopped and stood erect, staring at him. Sean smiled embarrassedly. The mother took her child by the hand and trotted away along the corridor to the staircase. Sean heard their scuffing feet and mutterings fade away.

He turned to go back into his room when he felt the give of something spongy under his foot. He froze. He moved his foot aside and looked down and saw that what he had trodden on was the head of the Sindy doll lying on the carpet. He thought of picking it up, or calling the mother and twin back, but didn't. Instead, he simply went into his room and shut the door.

46

He lay on the bed with his eyes closed. Maybe asleep. Maybe not.

A car engine growled outside as its ignition was switched on, tyres rasping on the gravel. Its headlights cast shadows round the room like a phantasmagoria as it did a U-turn and headed away up the gravel drive. One of the shadows it cast on the wall above the bed was the upside-down silhouette of a woman's headless torso, turning slowly in the air as if dangling by her feet.

Sean sat bolt upright with a gasp. Eyes wide, he shot looks all round him, and above him, craning his head back.

There was nothing on the wall. Just the normal shadows of the room in the spill of the floodlights and the light of the moon.

He looked over past the foot of the bed at the closed curtains.

He lifted himself off the bed and crossed to the window and slid up the bottom sash.

He leaned out and looked up above him first. The twins' window was closed and the curtains drawn. There was no light from inside.

He looked down. The faint spill of light from the hotel windows fell on the driveway, the occasional strand of party streamer fluttering on the surrounding bushes. A few stray balloons drifted across the pristine lawns to be gobbled up by the dark beyond the artificial lighting. Half in shadow sat a car with JUST MARRIED sprayed on it in shaving foam. He could see two youngish blokes tying a string of tin cans to its back bumper. They see Sean looking down at them and make a sibilant "Shshshsh!" in unison with fingers pressed to their lips.

"Sean? Sean?"

It was a woman's voice coming from below, out of sight. Where it coming from? It was familiar,

47

definitely. The first thing Sean thought was: it was the woman's voice he'd heard in the next room. God, it was her.

"Come on, Sean, you old fart! Don't you know how to have a good time? What's the matter with you?"

She was calling his name. Or was it *his* name? He shut the window, turned, looked for his hotel room key (hell, where was it? It was big enough, attached to that huge plastic tile), snatched it up in his fist and left his room like a whirlwind.

His name.

He tried to keep panic at bay, not knowing why he was panicking, not knowing why this voice, her voice, filled him with a sense of dread and excitement. He ran to the end of the corridor. The sign on the lift doors still said OUT OF ORDER. Shit. He took a right and hit the stairs, leaping, not afraid of the dark. There were other things to be afraid of than the dark.

Outside, the security light sprang on, brightly illuminating him like the searchlight in some old British prisoner of war movie, dazzling him slightly. He turned right and ran across the parking area to where the lights and the sound of the disco were blaring out. That was where the voice had been coming from, he was sure. That was where he could hear other voices now. That was where the woman was, he knew. He passed a guy in a morning suit and shirt unbuttoned at the neck throwing up in the undergrowth, two of his pals in top hats pretending to be looking after him but in fact more sozzled than he was. He saw another drunk man standing nearby, swigging Stella from a can.

"Excuse me," said Sean. "I'm looking for Sean. Is there a guy called Sean here tonight?"

"Sean? You're joking are you? Sean?" The pissed guy said, invading his personal space. "Sean's only the bloody *bridegroom*."

Swaying, he pointed to the huddle of young men with the one who was retching his guts up in the bushes. Sean knew the feeling. Bono and the Edge were bashing his head inside out from the function room. He went over to them, the youngsters. They looked too young to get married, all of them. Then he realised they were his age when he'd got married, and just as he realised that, they looked up at him. All except the one who was in a bad way, who remained bent over, his face in shadow, totally in shadow, hidden from Sean's view.

"Excuse me. Can I speak to Sean?"

"Who are you?"

"Are you Sean?"

"I'm the best man. Never mind me. Who the fuck are you?"

"I... Hey. No sweat. I just want to talk to Sean a minute..."

Sean moved forward, to ease past the bullet-headed best man and get a look at the vomiting kid's face. He needed to see that face. The best man didn't like Sean's hand on his arm and pushed back. Drink had made him belligerent. Sean hated that. He didn't like conflict at the best of times, but he didn't have any patience left any more. He put a hand against the man's chest and shoved him aside firmly and that should have been that, but the guy liked that even less and shoved back, harder. Next second they grabbed each other by the scruff of the shirt, lurching eyeball to eyeball. And Sean wasn't going to back down, not now, not tonight. He could rip the fucking guy's head off, if the truth be known. He was prepared for it, he was fucking ready to.

49

Then the kid, the bridegroom, looked up, right into Sean's face. And Sean's fist slackened on the best man's Moss Bros shirt. Because he didn't see Sean, didn't see *himself*, or anyone approximating himself. He saw a ginger-haired boy with bloodshot eyes and a pallor like death not even warmed up. The groom convulsed again as if reacting to an invisible kick in the stomach, the contents of which flew to the four winds, and he spun away, directing his monumental hughie at the geraniums.

"Sorry… Sorry mate," said Sean. "I thought you were somebody else. Sorry…"

He backed away, rapidly, hands up, but the best man and his mates had lost the lust for a fight and went back to nursing their bilious amigo.

On. Sean ran back inside. *Off.*

He headed straight up the stairs past the oil paintings – *look at all these photos, Sean* – the man in the ruff with the pointed beard and the woman with no eyebrows and three children. He froze mid-creak as he heard several woman laughing, and like a film going into reverse motion retraced his steps back to the reception area, listening.

The sound – he couldn't make out the words, just the voices, drunken, conspiratorial, disembodied for now – came from behind the door to the left of the reception desk. *Wives. Girlfriends. Women. Women will know. Women know everything*, he thought. Pictures went through his mind of high heels and chubby calves. Without pausing, he went through. He didn't know where the corridor went because he didn't read the sign with the arrows on. Doors led off, but the sound didn't come from any of them. There was a porthole-window at the far end and a strange sort of wavy light reflecting through it on the surrounding walls so he aimed for that and banged through it into chlorine and echo.

The hotel swimming pool was not exactly Olympic dimensions, but big enough for ladies who lunch to do the dog paddle and slag off their husbands. It was brightly lit from below the surface even at night – why at night? – the rippling lines of water dancing around the walls. He had the sense of a lava lamp flat-lining, and the unadorned surfaces deflected the tiniest sound back at him a hundredfold. It was deserted, except for an inflatable elephant and a pink and green rhinoceros with a gigantic air-filled tusk. The duo bobbed invitingly. The disco, distant, was belting out Tom Jones singing "Sex Bomb" now, which was all he needed.

"I've never been so sober in my life. Honest to God."

Sean turned to see that the woman's voice from before, the one he had heard all along, belonged to this girl, this bride, the one who was posing for the wedding photographer earlier, the one with flowers in her hair, bottle blonde, very much so, more than slightly overweight, didn't get it, slightly tarty-looking even in her white bridal dress too tight across the midriff, boobs like hostages, couldn't wait to get out of it, ready to get out of it. Drunk, drunk, drunk.

"I got married today." Sung up and down like a six-year-old.

"So I see," said Sean.

She swayed perilously. "I'm a married woman, me. I'm spoken for. It was my wedding day and everybody's got to give me a kiss!"

"I think you've had a little bit too much to drink, love. No offence."

She pulled a face. "What do you mean 'No offence?' Are you going to kiss me or not? I mean it now." She staggered towards him. One high heel on, one missing.

51

"All right. Calm down. OK. I don't know you, but – congratulations, OK?" Sean kissed her on the cheek, a glancing blow, as glancing as he could make it.

The bride grinned, then laughed.

She frowned. "What do you mean you don't know me?"

"I don't know you."

"On the lips. On the lips, it's got to be, or it doesn't count. All or nothing. Come on, it's my wedding day for Christ's sake!" She held out her arms at her side and twiddled her fingers, offering her mouth forward, eyes closed.

Sean kissed her on the lips. The bride didn't let him go. Her arms were round his neck. On his face. In his hair. She hung on for dear life, dear breath, sucking the air out of him. He thought of the inflated elephant. He wanted its air. He felt the sting of stale wine on her, on his tongue now. He had to pull her off his face like a limpet. As he held her at arm's-length he could see her blood-red lipstick smeared all over her chops. Her chest was heaving.

"That was all right, wasn't it?" she panted.

"No, not really."

He backed away, one hand keeping her at bay. She caught his arm and wrist and firmly planted it on one of her breasts. Sean snatched it away.

"No, seriously now. I'm serious," he said. He wanted to get away but she was coming at him, laughing.

"So am I. Look."

Sean followed her gaze down to where he saw that her frilly, insubstantial panty knickers had been pulled down to her ankles. He hadn't seen her doing it, but there they were. She laughed. She was grinning as she began to lift up her voluminous white wedding dress past her calves, the dimples of her knees, thighs…

Sean ran for the exit without looking back, but the bride kept lifting and kept laughing, he could see her lava-lamp shadows on the swimming pool walls, and for all he knew the elephant and rhino were laughing too because it sounded like the whole crowd at White Hart Lane shouting:

"Sean? *Sean!* SEAN!"

He ran until he could hear her no longer. He ran until he got her out of his head. This Sean, this *other* Sean she was calling rattled in his head. She was pissed. It was a coincidence. Plenty of people were called Sean. Get a grip, he told himself. What was he doing looking for an explanation when everyone was half cut? He had to wait till morning. Things would make sense in the morning. They had to. He tasted her cheap Chardonnay on his tongue again and squirmed inside. He could feel her sweaty hands over his neck and in his hair. He reached the door to his hotel room, Room 24, and fumbled with his key in the lock.

A clunk made him stop. The clunk of closing doors, below. A grinding machine noise wound and cogged into vertical action. He recognized it with no effort at all. It was the unmistakable sound of the lift ascending from the ground floor. He turned and looked down to the far end of the corridor, and he knew what he would see.

OUT OF ORDER.

The lift doors still displayed the sign.

The disco throbbed in the ventricles of his heart.

He fixated on those words, on those letters.

OUT OF ORDER.

Somehow he couldn't look away, though his hand was still on his room key and all he had to do was to turn it. He couldn't look away. An ice-coldness swept up from his belly and he knew if it reached his head he might collapse. When the coldness reached the floor his brain was on, that would be it, oh God, and he could hear the mechanism as it rose up the shaft. And he imagined the digital blink of the numbers, innocent numbers, blameless numbers, rising. Alarm clock numbers. Wake, please wake, please wake.

OUT OF ORDER.

Doors opening.

His exact double was standing there in the lift. The "other" Sean. Leaning casually in the insipid yellow down-light of the lift, dressed to the nines in a snooker player's tuxedo and bow tie, with a heavy black overcoat slung over his arm, smuggest of smiles on his face. Face disappearing as the doors slid shut.

OUT OF ORDER.

Sean waited for the ice to hit. It didn't. His blood boiled. He was galvanized, suddenly. He flew down the corridor at the lift, like a crazy person, hammering his fists on the lift doors, then trying to prise them open, pressing the hook of his fingers into the crack between them, uselessly. Then, hearing its smuggest of hums, smuggest of descents, started thumbing and bashing all the buttons to no effect.

Suddenly the hum stopped. He looked down. He saw that indicator light had stopped on number "1." He heard the lift doors open on the floor below. He ran to the stairs and didn't stop.

He burst into the first-floor corridor from the stairwell just as the lift doors were unhurriedly closing. He jammed in hands, wincing as they crushed them for a second, then, blocked, pause a beat, then re-open. He stood his ground. Tightened his fists.

But the lift was empty.

Of course it was empty.

He turned and looked down the length of the empty corridor. It was in darkness except for a single, nondescript FIRE EXIT sign. He saw something on the floor.

He walked over to it, knelt down, and picked it up in his fingers. His shadow cast by the FIRE EXIT light was long, the whole length of the corridor, and not man-shaped any more.

The object he touched was a square of blue chalk. The sort that snooker players use.

The sudden loud clack of two snooker balls hitting. Reverberating. His head jerked up as if yanked on a rope.

The door only two feet away from him was marked "GAMES ROOM".

He stood up and moved towards it. The floor felt tacky and glued to his feet, holding him back. He gripped the door handle. He could hear the sound of *his own* laughter coming from inside the room. *Was* it his own? Why was he even questioning this? He couldn't pause, he couldn't stop now. He opened the door.

The only lighting was the downward-pitched cone from a shade overhanging the autopsy slab of green baize. It illuminated at the very edge of its circumference a big fat half-spent Monte Cristo, resting on the rim of an ashtray on the mahogany surround. Its tip did not glow, but Sean could see smoke rising from it with lugubrious insouciance.

He walked slowly to the billiard table, his eyes fixed on the smoking cigar. He could hear only his own breathing. He was waiting for his eyes to become accustomed to the dark, but that wasn't happening. He passed a snooker cue and a variety of balls arranged on the green baize like a still life. Like atoms. Like DNA. He thought of his own DNA. Of life. Of Ali's life. As he stared at the green baize, he saw what looked like the perfectly round shadow of a large coin. He thought of the tip he should have given the driver. The memory of Ali's teasing made his throat feel raw. As he looked closer, he began to hear a quiet bip… bip… bip… bip… bip…

Mesmerized, he reached out the flat of his hand to touch it, to pick it up, if he could pick it up, but the minute his hand hovered over it – bip…

A splash of red daubed the back of his hand. Bright red. He snatched it back, stupidly, as if he could make it un-happen.

He stared at it, not wanting to touch it, not wanting to smear it, though he knew what it was he didn't want it confirmed. His breath passed quickly through his teeth and back again in quick succession. His chest turned to lead.

His eyes jumped up to the light fitting, the shade, and the chain holding it up at each end. Without thinking, he reached up to the nearest chain and ran his fingers up it and examined them.

His fingers were covered in blood. DNA. Life.

The cigar smoke caught like razors at the back of his throat.

Bip… bip…

He looked up at the ceiling fitting. He could make out what he first thought was a shadow – shadow of what? – but then realised was a huge dark, black stain up there, three feet wide.

"Oh my God."

He cannoned out of the games room, bouncing off the far wall, and shot for the stairs ignoring the pain in his crushed shoulder. Physical pain was the least of his worries. He couldn't give a shit about *that*. Half flying, half stumbling, he raced up the steps back to the second floor.

He exploded through the double doors and charged, breathless, to the room directly above – his room, Room 24. He thrust his hand deep in his pocket for the key.

It was only then the realised the door was already wide open.

His fingers clasped round the key in his pocket tightly, anyway. Making a fist. He was unable to extract it.

Wide open.

Inside, a store window dummy, no, a suit, no, the manager was standing in the middle of the room, wearing on his head a red fez, streamers bedecking his shoulders, bright coloured streamers, it didn't make sense. It did make sense. The decorations strewn from the wedding reception. He was looking at Sean expectantly. He'd heard his footsteps approaching. He wasn't surprised to see him, but there was something about his expression, something Sean wanted to look away from, he didn't know why.

"Mr Merritt. I'm sorry."

Sean walked into his own hotel room.

"What's going on?"

"You didn't answer the telephone. I knocked the door and there was no answer…"

Sean dropped to his knees and, finding a join, tore up the carpet that lay over the spot on the floor which he reckoned was above the shadow. The stain. The blood.

"What are you doing in my room?"

"Somebody complained. About the noise. Naturally we…"

There was nothing on the outside of the carpet and nothing on the underside. He folded it back. The tan underlay was pristine too.

"What kind of noise?"

"Er… Well, I'm… Voices."

Sean pulled up the underlay, popping the tacks, tearing it mercilessly. There was no sign of a stain on it or underneath it on the bare floorboards.

"What kind of voices?"

The manager shifted embarrassedly from foot to foot.

"Having it off," said Sean. "Is that what you're telling me? Making love? Having sex? Screwing? Fucking?"

The manager laughed lightly in acknowledgement. He remembered he was wearing the fez and took it off, reverentially, undertaker-like, and flicked away the inappropriate streamers. Inappropriate to his own discomfort.

"What's that?" said Sean.

The manager turned to look at what Sean was staring at. An overnight bag sat on the slatted luggage table beside the vanity mirror. A two-tone leather overnight bag that Sean didn't recognize.

"What's that doing there? It's not mine."

The manager walked over to it and examined the leather tag.

"It does have your name and address on it, sir. 'S. Merritt, 3 Kay's Road, Finsbury Park…' "

Sean was suddenly aware for the first time that the bathroom taps were running, just like they were running when Ali disappeared. The sound was identical.

"Did you turn the taps on?" he asked the manager, hardly waiting a beat for the answer. "Did you turn the bathroom taps on?"

"No, sir. They were on when I came in."

Sean spun round, taking in the rest of the room, what else was here that shouldn't be here, what else was wrong. The lead-heavy feeling in his chest came back with a vengeance. He saw the room service trolley sitting there, just like the one Monica had wheeled in when they'd had their chat. He went to it. The plate was uncovered, the napkin screwed in a ball, the meal eaten – apart from seven hollow pink tiger prawn shells. He reeled back to the manager. And the two-tone overnight bag.

"Open it."

The manager looked at him.

"Open it."

The manager carefully lifted the bag from the rest and put it on the bed. The bed bounced slightly. The manager folded down the loop handles and slowly pulled the tag of the zip along the length of the top. It rasped in fits and starts, got stuck and he had to ease it on with a bit of manual dexterity and persuasion. His fingers were quite female, Sean noticed. Quite like a surgeon opening a wound.

The manager stepped back from it and looked at Sean. Sean was not about to take over. He could continue, thank you very much. Sean's eyes told him as much. Sean was the one who was terrified, but the manager was the one with beads of sweat in big dots on the back of his neck. Sean stood behind him as the man arched his head forward and looked into the wound.

The manager laughed through his nose. Sean's face didn't show any sign of relief as he moved round to see for himself. The manager was holding up a red snooker ball which had been nestled within, in a bed of white fluffy towels.

His smile faded as he looked back in the bag, taking out one of the fluffy towels. Head bent over, he froze in mid-motion, staring. Sean thought he heard him emit a little whimper. Perhaps that was his imagination but it wasn't his imagination when he watched the man backing away with his hand covering his mouth, stuffed against his teeth.

Sean stood in place of him over the overnight bag, denying the sickening dread that was rising inside. He placed a hand on each side, looping thumbs under each lip, and tugged open the mouth of it.

Ali stared up at him, her severed head neatly packed inside the leather case, love long gone from her staring dead marbles of eyes, an obscenely neat curl falling across her forehead as an added insult, not a mark on her cheeks or perfect skin, a white billiard ball rammed deep in her mouth, filling it, filling her, filling his throat too.

The SOCO team were all over the games room in their white astronaut-type gear, white paper suits and baby-big shoes, dusting the snooker table and light fittings for fingerprints, using their science fiction black light tubes to detect any blood stains; all the stuff you saw on *Waking the Dead* every week. The difference was, Sean thought, you couldn't sit back and enjoy this. There wasn't a neat solution staring you in the face. You couldn't open a beer or go for a pee. You were *in* this. Your wife was dead and her blood was on your hands. In your skin, in your pores. And some policeman with a swagger and ill-advised sideburns was carrying the overnight bag in his outstretched arms to a vehicle with black windows. And you were sitting in a straight backed chair, with a mug of hot tea in your hands.

The woman DI thought he looked as if he had gone without sleep for a week. It was her first observation. Don't people go mad if they do without sleep? Don't they become paranoid and do crazy things if their circadian rhythms are disrupted? He'd drained to the colour of a Belfast sink, which didn't mean he was innocent. It didn't mean he was guilty. She thought about the woman whose head had been taken away, not Sean. She couldn't give a damn about Sean. She gave a damn about the killer.

The doctor confided in her, in as low a whisper as he could manage: "Go easy on him. He's in a state of shock."

"Join the club," she responded through pursed lips.

Her beefy detective sergeant watched a Scene of Crime officer carefully pick up a half-smoked cigar using tweezers and drop it into an evidence bag.

In the manager's office, later, Sean put the empty mug on the desk in front of him. The tea had curdled a small part of him that wasn't curdled already. He felt vague. He felt dulled, dim, semi-absent. Already he wanted them to leave him alone and they hadn't even begun. He didn't even want them to open their mouths, if it meant he had to open his.

"I'm sorry we have to ask you some questions, Mr Merritt," said the DI, not unpleasantly. She had a good bedside manner. *Corpse-side manner.* It reminded Sean of the calm reassurance of a newsreader. Not that he was reassured at all.

"I know it must be distressing at this time," said her DS. "But I'm sure you want us to do our job." Sean thought he had the look of a rugger player and pint merchant and instantly felt the bloke wasn't on his side. He didn't think *anybody* was on his side. Why the hell should they be? He rubbed his head, having trouble dragging himself into the moment, having *real* trouble with that. Wanting it all to go, go away, please, somehow just –

"Can you tell us…" said the woman DI softly. He thought of a woman politician but couldn't remember her name. "Can you remember anything, however trivial, about this man you followed to the games room?"

Sean shook his head, trying to shake some reality into it, too, if he could. He rubbed his eyes and fell short of slapping his own cheeks. *Concentrate. They're trying to*

61

help you. Are they trying to help you? What's easier for them, helping you or –

"Had you ever seen the overnight bag before?"

Sean shook his head again.

The DS placed a clear plastic bag on the hotel manager's desk. When Sean looked at it he saw that there was a luggage label inside.

"You didn't write this label?"

"No."

"This is your handwriting, sir?"

"Look. I didn't do it. You think I could do that? To my wife?"

"Take it easy, sir," said the rugger bugger, as if the reaction came straight from training school, chapter three, page thirty. "We're not accusing you of anything."

Oh. *Right.*

Sean stared blankly as the spot he had chosen on the wall, a little bit of damp rot. It served its purpose well. He felt quite safe as long as his eyes didn't drift too far away from it and the enormity of the whole damn world fell about his ears. Hold it. Hold that damp spot, that's it. Tickling sounds and reminders of the hotel filtered in from afar and only made him shiver because he felt completely elsewhere now. He felt he was in the Arctic. His teeth were chattering like those wind-up Hallowe'en skulls. He wanted to put a fire on, he wanted to switch on that four bar electric fire, but was afraid to ask. And suddenly waiting in the chasm for their next question was too much to bear.

"It was him," he said, then repeated it slightly louder for their benefit, in case they hadn't heard. "It was *him*."

In the en suite bathroom, Sean revolved under the spray of the shower, his fingers combing through his hair. *En suite*. Eyes closed, he washed soapsuds from all over his body, trying to let the spray relax him. That's the way he'd been taught; water, switch the shower off, lather up all over, then water to wash it off. He thought it was a penny-pinching habit from his father, to save water, or from his Dad's time in National Service. But habits, even stupid habits, were hard to break. His pores. His skin. His fingertips. He needed them to feel cleansed. It was when he finally switched off the shower he heard a knock at the hotel room door. He wondered if someone had been knocking a while. He stepped out of the cubicle and wrapped a "Shewstone House" towel round his waist. His wetness began to be absorbed into it.

His dripping feet left footprints into the plush carpet. He used a smaller towel to dry his hair. He opened the door. It was Monica. In civvies rather than white blouse, black shirt waitress gear this time. She wore chino trousers, fatigue style with more pockets than anybody but a forester would need, and a T-shirt under a purple Creighton Prep hoodie. He let her in without saying a word. Her hair wasn't tied back now and he saw it came to her shoulders, and had a touch of auburn in it which he couldn't tell was natural or not, but it went with her light dusting of freckles.

He noticed her register his suitcase which lay open on the bed.

"What happened?"

"They let me go," he sighed. "God knows why. It's all a bit of a blur... I didn't hear half of what they were saying, to be honest."

She sat with her back to the vanity mirror, knees together.

"What did you tell them?"

Sean shrugged. "What *could* I tell them? That there's a man out there who looks like me – *exactly* like me?" He continued packing as he talked. " 'What does this man look like, sir?' 'Oh, he's my height, my build, my colour hair, my colour eyes, he's got a mole here, he's got a scar here from falling off a swing when he was six years old, he's got a wedding ring here…' "

The horror crept up on him again. He ran out of words and fetched his soap bag from the bathroom. Pressed it flat in the case.

"I'm sorry." She really sounded like she meant it. Sorry for being a pain, sorry for disbelieving you.

He shook his head. "It's not your fault."

"What did they say?"

"At the end of it all? They said, 'Go home, sir.' Just like that. They said they'd give me counselling, was what they said." Anger rose in him now. "I don't want counselling. I want my…" He bit his tongue. Having crept up on him, it pounced. The word. The horror dug in its fangs. He didn't want to show her that, and kept facing his suitcase, bare shoulders hunched.

She could see the sadness in him. You didn't have to see it, it was palpable. He was all alone with it and she didn't think she could step into that bubble. It wasn't her place to, and he didn't want it. But the truth was, he might want to be alone, but she didn't. But she wasn't strong enough to stay.

"I'll go. I…"

He didn't protest. She walked silently to the door and opened it, and then heard him say:

"No don't. Please… Don't go."

It was what she wanted to hear him say, so much so that for a second she thought it was only in her head.

Bored. Sean was bored now. He'd sat for hours and he'd run through his story a hundred times for them. What more did they want to hear? Did they want him to repeat it and repeat it until he made some slip up and they could slam the handcuffs on? Or did they genuinely want to know the truth? It didn't seem like it.

"It wasn't me. I've said it till I'm blue in the bloody *toes*."

"It's this man, who looks like you." The DS made a grimace, a plea to make it easier for them.

"Like Dr Jekyll and Mr Hyde," said the woman DI, momentarily thoughtful and momentarily sympathetic. "So you're the 'good' you, and the other one is the 'bad' you?" She took out a pack of cigarettes and offered Sean one.

"It's not allowed, inside the building."

She shrugged. "Let's bend the rules. Shall we?"

He shook his head. "I don't smoke."

"Don't you? Never?"

"Never have. Ever."

She put the packet away, without having one herself.

The sergeant leaned forward, fingers woven together on the desk and thumbs making a little steeple. "There was this old episode of *Star Trek*. When there was a fault in the transporter, and it produced a good Captain Kirk and a bad Captain Kirk? That sort of thing?" He was milking it for every ounce of sarcasm, the twat.

Sean kept that thought to himself. "I know it sounds mad. I know that."

The sarcasm went. The Rottweiler arrived. "What are you playing at, Sean, eh?" It was going to have his arm off.

"I'm not 'playing at' anything! Do you honestly think I'd make this up?"

"'It wasn't me, it was somebody who looked like me.' Come on, mate. Fifty per cent of the prison population of the UK have that catchy little ditty tattooed across their foreheads."

"I know – I *know!*"

"So what's his motive, this double of yours?" said the woman DI. "Why should he want to murder your wife?"

Sean's brain was working overtime. It was question he hadn't asked himself. Why hadn't he asked himself that? He couldn't believe it. His eyes were flickering. *Wait a minute.* They watched the cogs turning. They weren't going to give him forever. Then the only *possible* truth dawned on him and it came as such a revelation it made him grin.

"He wants to replace me. It's so bloody obvious, why didn't I think of it before? That's what it is. That's why he's setting me up. That's it. He wants to *replace* me."

Which was exactly when the woman DI wished she was home with her husband and kids in front of the TV with her feet up and some hot cocoa, and became absolutely convinced that Sean Merritt was mad.

Sean methodically pressed his folded clothes into the suitcase. Then he carried over Ali's clothes too and did the same. He arranged them carefully, not wanting to get them wrinkled, and ran the flat of his hands over them to make sure.

"You'll have to tell them, Sean," said Monica, but he didn't look up. "You know. Tell them the truth."

He didn't move. "The truth? What good is that? It won't bring Ali back, will it? What does it matter who believes what? What does it matter if he did it, or I did it, or…"

He stared down at the summer dress in his hands, the one with big sunflower heads all over it, the one she always took on holiday. Spain. Portugal. Italy. *That restaurant in Positano at the sea front where they brought out the giant fish and we got talking to that nice American couple, and those backpackers introduced us to limoncello.*

"You know, she always thought this one made her look fat. Fat? She never looked fat. She always looked…" His voice splintered. "Stunning…"

He swallowed the feelings, went and steadied himself against the wardrobe. Monica walked over and rested her hands on his bare, wet back. She put her arms around his body, round his waist and round his shoulders, holding him tight.

"It's all right. It's all right."

She kissed his skin as his shoulders heaved with sobs, holding back tears herself.

The woman DI poured fresh tea supplied by the hotel restaurant. The waiter with a Tintin haircut and surplus collar exited, reminding Sean of the normality waiting agonisingly close outside the manager's office door.

"So this man. This double…" said the DI. "If he wants to replace you, why didn't he kill you?"

"I don't know! I don't have the rule book. Maybe he *can't* kill me. If he kills me he destroys himself."

"So if you die, he dies."

"I don't know. You keep asking me and I keep telling you – I don't know!"

"You did it, didn't you?" said the triple-chinned DS matter-of-factly. "Took her out, into the woods round here somewhere. Brought back your nasty little trophy in the overnight bag. Dreamed up this nutty little concoction – "

"No. No. No!" screamed Sean, finally losing it, not unreasonably, he thought. "It was him! You should be out there looking for *him!*" His fists banged the desk like an infant in a tantrum but he didn't give a shit any more. The door opened and a uniform WPC looked in.

"Bring the car round, Wendy," said the woman DI without flinching. "Me laddo is coming with us."

M onica left him and crossed the room, to get tissues from the box on the vanity mirror. She heard the crunching of footsteps on the gravel of the drive, and as she plucked at each Kleenex she saw through the window in front of her a woman in a police uniform walking off briskly towards a parked police car. She returned to Sean and pressed the tissues into his hand. He hadn't moved. He blew into them and folded them into an ever smaller, tighter square. He turned and looked at the suitcase.

"What are you going to do?"

He tossed the tissue into a bin. "Go home. What's left of my home. Tell the girls. Somehow. God knows how. I have to leave now. Except – I…" He paused. "I never like travelling alone."

Monica smiled. She knew what she was being asked, and as she was thinking about it she turned to look out of the window again, faintly aware that there was more activity outside. Voices, not loud. Police, gesturing, she now saw. Then something in his voice in the way he said "I never like travelling alone," the innuendo of it, the bluntness of it, the selfish-tinged out-of-characterness of it, made her turn back to him.

He was sitting on the bed next to his open suitcase. It was still half empty. He was just sitting there, immobile. Stopped.

"Have you finished packing?"

"Not quite," he said, without looking at her and without blinking. Then he did look up at her, still unblinking, as if he knew what she was thinking – exactly what she was thinking – and answered her by taking out a packet of Silk Cut from the bedside table, taking a lighter from inside it and lighting one up.

Monica felt a slackness in her bladder and a lack of willpower in the muscles of her legs. Just when she needed them. But she also thought, almost comically: *No swift moves.* She was justifying the fact that she was rooted to the spot. Cars and footsteps sounded on the far side of the window but she was inside, and she could have spun round and leapt at that window but she had to keep her eyes on Sean's double because he was already coming, already had the flat of his hand (and it hurt, hurt came back to her) over her mouth – hard, so hard her own teeth drew blood, salt sweet on her tongue as he shoved her back against the wall.

While they ushered Sean out of the manager's office, the DS said to his guv'nor: "I'll radio we're on our way." His face had the repulsive, confident smirk of a match-winning hooligan. Sean didn't know why they didn't high five or punch the air shouting "Result!" or whoop, like the audience on *Jerry Springer*. If they were fitting him up as some kind of Jill Dando homicidal maniac, why couldn't they at least *enjoy* it, for Christ's sake? Why the pretence that this was some by the book, rational enquiry? He almost wanted to do one of those whoops himself, just to wind them up.

"Look, look…" he was saying to the woman DI as a phone rang on the reception desk. "I can prove it to you! You'll realise it *has* to be my double. Look, look, look…" He took out the envelope, took out the passport photo of Ali. "He stole this off me. Took it from my wallet when I wasn't in my room." He showed them the two thumb prints, one in blood, one in dirt. "This is me, and this is him. Look. Identical. Me. *Him*. Not similar. *Identical!* Look. Explain that. Go on, explain it! You *can't!*"

"Sean Merritt, I believe you are responsible for the murder of your wife Alison Merritt. I am arresting you. You do not have to say anything but anything you do say will be…"

But even as he was listening to the caution, he was listening to the girl on reception as she said: "Reception. Certainly, Mr Merritt. I'll have the bill made out and waiting for you. Thank you."

Sean felt an out of body experience.

"…you later rely on in court. Anything you do say may be…"

Sean jerked the hands off his elbows.

"He's here. Shut up! – he's *here!*"

Upstairs, the man who looked like Sean gently placed the receiver down on its cradle. His body, still glistening with water from the shower, was tensed, every muscle taut as an anatomical drawing, a flayed man, a Saint Bartholomew, same Christian martyr beyond-it-all expression. Not of this world. Above it, looking down. Looking down at Monica, held face down by his other hand in the pillow, held by the back of the neck, strong enough to snap it. When the phone had pinged he pulled her up, the way someone lifts a cat by the scruff of the neck and the poor thing is immobilised and scared, and

70

with unhurried pleasure forced the leeches of his lips onto hers.

Sean grabbed the detective sergeant by the lapels – thank God for policemen wearing suits – and threw him, full force, catching him off-balance, at the woman DI who sprawled backwards as Sean leapt in the other direction, upstairs.

"Stop him! Don't let him get out!"

The girl receptionist looked blank. A duty manager stood behind her and comprehended, or at least took the initiative, and pressed a button which locked the glass front door with a *ker-clunk*. The WPC outside, returning to the hotel, pressed against glass, found that she was faced by an immovable object.

In Room 24, Monica thrashed against Sean's double, even knowing as she did so it was futile. Women were weak, she thought, and she was weaker than most. Physically anyway. She could do not much more than a drowning kitten could scratch. Her foot lashed out at the bedside table, bang, bang, sending the book and lamp and clock radio cascading, wrecked.

Sean zig-zagged up the stairs, knocking the old paintings – *photos* – askew. He tripped up, fell to his knees. The manager stood in front of him, looming over him, and he could hear the girl receptionist was coming up the stairs after him. Sean elbowed the manager hard in the groin, doubling him up, and barged past him, leaving him as a lurching obstacle for his other pursuers.

A hacksaw flew across the carpet, knocked by Monica from Sean's double's hand. He forced Monica down on the bed. Onto the suitcase. Her hands grasped for something – anything. She lifted a canister of shaving foam and struck him on the forehead. It seemed to make no difference. He grabbed her wrist and twisted it, forcing it out of her hand. It bounced away across the bed.

Sean burst through the swing doors to the corridor that led to Room 24, caught immediately off guard by the sight of the twin girls, in pyjamas, fooling around, play-fighting, one laughing uproariously while the other wore a large Elastoplast over her mouth. Two identical, pigtailed heads turned. When they saw him they froze, and ran away. Panting, Sean tore the DO NOT DISTURB card off the door handle of his room. He opened the door. Tried to. It was locked.

Incensed, Sean's double yanked the suitcase away from Monica on the bed. It spilled its contents all over the floor. He slapped her hard across the side of the face. She reeled back, stunned.

Sean hammered on the door with his fists. It was no good. He stepped back and took a good run at it, using his shoulder as a battering ram (like they do in stupid films) which didn't work, (stupidly, stupid), then tried with his foot.

He burst in, sprawling into the room, shoulder hitting the wall to see

to see

to see – *HIMSELF.*

HIMSELF strangling Monica.

– to see Monica, her clothes torn and disheveled, sprawled across the bed, head upside down hanging over the edge of it, with HIMSELF sitting across her, legs apart, across her hips, HIMSELF posed as if riding her, the rim of the bath towel pushing down on her, HIMSELF with his arms outstretched downwards, squeezing the life out of her tiny throat. Her flicking eyes rolling up into her skull as if looking for something up there long lost, the gurgle in her throat saying, no not there, no not there.

And his double looked up at him.

Straight into Sean eyes. His own eyes.

And Sean stared back as the laughter of his own voice rang mockingly in his ears. Monica's last breath had long departed her body.

Sean stared at the scene, with no capacity to act, only to speak.

"I'm going mad. I'm going mad," he said.

And his doppelganager smiled with teeth just as imperfect and off-white at Sean's own, still with Monica in his vice-like maniacal grip and not letting go, and chuckled to himself in plain delight at his knowledge:

"No you're not," said Sean's double. "You're mad already."

Absolute, unconditional horror played plasticine with Sean's features as the blood drained from his face. He was going out of body again, and in a bad way. And in less than a breath it had happened and was over, with no tripping a switch and no cutting of a cord and no scream of alarm. And now he was sitting astride her, looking down at Monica beneath him, stretched away from him, chin in the air, bones of her breastbone countable. The U of the middle of her collarbone. He was looking down at his own hands fastened round on her tiny throat, his own hands not letting go. The beads of bath water dotting his own forearms. Finding himself half-naked now, and crouched on his own bed in the body of a murderer.

He looked up startled to where he had been standing, across the room, looking at the bed. He wanted reality to rescue him but it didn't. There was no-one standing there, where he once was. How could there be? There was no Sean any more. *Bye bye Sean.*

"No."

He was across her, fully dressed now, wearing the clothes he was wearing downstairs while he was being interviewed by the police and it popped into his head, this phrase as if someone whispered it. *The old switcheroo.*

73

And he thought of the leering sadistic grin that had been on the man's face, on his face, and it made his own melt like candle wax. He was a blob but he was Sean. He *was* Sean; but who *the fuck* was he *now*?

"*The old switcheroo, matey.*"

"No," said Sean. At least he knew his voice was still his. "No. *No…*"

The door to Room 24 slammed open. Sean was looking down at his upturned confessing murderous helpless hands. *Someone's* hands. And before he could even look up at who had burst in, they were snatched away. The assistant manager and the girl receptionist were on top of him like a couple of representatives of some Worldwide Fund for Wrestlers Convention. Hurting him. *Leave it out!* Twisting his elbows up behind his back, overpowering him, throwing him off his bed onto the carpet. The air was instantly knocked out of him and he couldn't get any back in. Flashes went off like fireworks, poked at his eyes. He felt a forearm heavy as a railway sleeper across the back of his neck. *Now, before I… is somebody going to tell me what the… what the…*

Sideways, from Shake-n-Vac level (getting into his nostrils big-time), Monica jerked upright, hand to her throat, retching, gagging for breath like a cat with a hairball. The manager entered Sean's screwy comic-strip point of view, fussing to help her. Sean heard him say to her: "I told you, you idiot!" Then, looking down at Sean with a shine of spittle on his lower lip. "Bastard! You bastard!"

"Don't fight it, Sean," said the chubby girl receptionist. "You know not to fight it, don't you?" And Sean stared up as she held up a giant syringe, needle pointing towards the ceiling, and whipped off the sterile cover. He knew where that needle was going and he didn't like it, but the poxy, beige assistant manager was a

74

dead weight on his back. The girl vanished and he felt this sudden spike dig deep in his left buttock, and though he roared he knew it would do fuck-all good, and even as he bared his teeth he felt a warm feeling spread through his muscles and knew that temporarily at least he was kissing this world goodbye, whether he liked it or not.

When his eyes opened, Sean found himself lying alone on the bed in the same room, fully dressed, waking from a deep, untroubled sleep, the best he'd had in years, as if nothing – *nothing* – had happened. *It was all a dream, a nightmare.* Was it? The corniest of movie clichés, made real? Even as he was feeling it he wondered why his sense of freedom, relief and elation was cancelled out by a seeping feeling of dread. All was not right. Or was it? *Don't knock it, son*, he thought. He heard the warm, far off phuttering of the lawn mower, the twitter-tweet of songbirds hopping from branch to branch. Ornithology was good, he remembered. Ornithology was great. He ran his tongue over his lips, and found they were unnaturally dry.

He sat up, swaying slightly on the edge of the bed, trying very precisely to work out what he had imagined and what he hadn't. But the main thing was, he told himself, he was *here*, and he was *safe*. The room was as he last saw it. His feet were square on the floor, he felt completely calm and unhurt, and even peaceful. Yes, sod it, peaceful.

"How are you, Sean?"

It was Monica's voice, but Monica wasn't in the room.

He slowly stood and revolved on the spot, looking into every corner of the room. But there was nobody there but him. If it wasn't coming from the room, he thought, maybe it was coming from inside his head.

"How are you now?"

This time he could tell where it was coming from. He walked over to the ornate mirror, the large Louis Whatever one that dominated one wall, and touched the cheek of his own worried-looking reflection. He didn't know whether to be reassured that his reflection was there, behind glass, where it belonged, or –

"Are you feeling angry at me?" said Monica's voice. "Those are your real feelings, Sean. Don't deny your real feelings."

*I*n the observation room, Monica switched off the microphone. The hotel manager stood next to her, chewing a thumbnail, wearing a shabby Fair Isle sweater and cord trousers. She herself no longer wore the waitress uniform but a slate grey business suit, and a neck brace fastened round her neck. The two of them watched Sean standing in the antiseptically-plain, institutional hospital room beyond, touching the glass of the mirror on the other side.

"I've prescribed chlorpromazine for the anxiety and restlessness," said the manager. "Seventy-five mil a day."

Monica frowned. "And have him doped up like a nice little zombie?"

"Look what he did to you."

She rubbed her neck. "He's my patient. I don't want to fight to see his symptoms through some anti-psychotic fog."

She stepped out of the room into the plain, lime green corridor of the hospital, with its many identical doors *leading off. She had learned by now not to be distracted or disturbed by the patients' peculiar behaviour but adopted the requisite benign smile. Anything else might be interpreted as invasive or inappropriate and you never know what might accidentally set them off. It was a steep learning curve. Professor Dumbledore stood muttering to himself, flitting his hands over each other as if trying to catch a mouse. Germaine Greer sat on a windowsill, sobbing over some long lost childhood pet, or the long lost childhood itself. It was best not to dwell on the awful crimes these people had committed, and concentrate on their care. The girl from reception was kneeling on the floor, doing her best to comfort the woman.*

"Nurse," said the hotel manager, behind her. "She shouldn't be out of her room. You know too much human contact winds her up."

"Sorry, doctor. She wanted to."

Monica fetched a can of Lilt from the vending machine.

"There was a perceptual leap," she said to her male colleague, returning to the subject of Sean Merritt as she pulled its tab. "A sensory switching to the autoscopic self." She sipped. "It could be the turning point."

"He's a lost cause, Monica."

"He's a lost soul, Paul. But he's not a lost cause," she said.

Sean looked at her as she came in and sat opposite him. She was in that same ubiquitous black-and-white waitress uniform. He wondered why waitresses all dressed like that, like it was some kind of European Union directive, the "bistro imperative" or something. He was both relieved to see her again, and irritated. He stopped his fists bunching. He didn't want to show her the extent of his pent-up anger. He didn't move from the hotel room bed and she took residence in the repro Georgian chair by the vanity table. A manila folder rested on her crossed knees, bending slightly, and she made no attempt to talk for a long while. Sean thought two could play at that game. He had a million questions to ask but he was damned if he was going to give her the satisfaction of asking them.

Eventually she gave in, and the first question came from her, when her twiddling ballpoint pen finally came to rest on the folder.

"What's my name, Sean?"

Sean thought it must be a trick question, and not a very subtle one at that, but he wasn't in the mood to play games any more.

"Monica, of course."

He stared at her. The door opened and the barman, the second barman, entered carrying a VCR machine. Monica nodded. The man knelt down and set about connecting it to the TV set in the corner.

"Who am I, Sean?" she repeated. "What do I do?"

"You're a waitress." Sean snorted a laugh, but there was enough sour apathy loaded into his reply without that addendum.

"My name is Dr Monica Chase, Sean. I'm a psychiatrist."

"Don't be stupid."

She leaned forward.

"What happened when you attacked me, Sean?"

"*He* attacked you."

"*You* attacked me. You know that, don't you? You felt it. Something happened in your mind. It wasn't him, was it? It was you."

The barman stood to one side of the television set with his arms compactly folded. His belly made his shirt ride up at the front like a valance. He was squat, shaven-headed and strong-looking and it struck Sean that he was now in the role of some kind of heavy in case of trouble.

He thumbed towards the newcomer. "What's the barman doing here?" Nobody said anything. Sean was getting pissed off now. They were letting him do all the running and not giving anything in return. "What's going on? Tell me."

"Are you ready for this, Sean? I think you are."

She took out a VCR and slid it into the rectangular mouth of the player. She picked up the remote control from the top of the set, quickly familiarized herself with the buttons, and pressed "Play."

Monica knew the footage well. CCTV images filmed by security cameras located in various positions all round the building, bleached and blurred in a hundred shades of grey, six-digit time-code running across the bottom of the screen. First shot, a high angle of the iron gates opening electronically, to allow a square, high security vehicle through. Closing after the van has entered. Cut to another camera angle. The square black van, a police vehicle, pulling up outside the entrance. The vault-thick metal doors swinging open at the back. Sean stepping out of it, escorted by two police officers, wearing dark uniforms and peaked caps, into the building. Handcuffed.

"Tell me what you see, Sean."

Sean watched. Thinking it an infantile exercise, he ran his hand through his hair, but for her stupid benefit, described what he saw:

"I'm arriving at the hotel. With Ali. In the courtesy mini-bus."

Monica knew what the next shot was. Inside, at the admissions desk, where Paul Davenish, the residential

79

psych at the unit for the last five years, first talked to his new patient. Ali was not there on screen, even though Sean could be clearly seen talking to thin air as if someone was standing next to him.

"Me. And Ali…" Sean said. "Talking to the hotel manager. All that Visa business…"

Next shot, the hospital canteen. This one always filled Monica with sadness, she couldn't help it. There was something heartstring-pulling about her patient sitting there and eating alone. Talking to thin air, chuckling to himself as if he were enjoying a romantic meal for two. He seemed so happy that night, she thought. Oblivious to the other mostly doped-up inmates in the canteen all round him. He only had eyes for someone who wasn't even there.

Sean smiled as the memory came back to him. "I'm with Ali in the restaurant. We're joking about the other guests. Having a good old laugh."

Monica watched his expression. She'd have sworn his face filled with a feeling roughly approximating as love, but she knew better than to let that fool her.

Other shots continued in sequence. She knew them by heart. Sean sleeping in his room, tossing and turning. Alone. Occasionally visiting the bathroom. Occasionally holding imaginary conversations with someone on the bed, gesticulating, then nudging up tenderly. Then, later, according to the time code, Sean pacing up and down, with his hand to his face, but no mobile held in it.

"I'm phoning the girls," he said.

Another CCTV camera angle. "The nymphomaniac in the wedding dress." On the screen, Sean was reacting to the invisible advances of the drunken bride, pawing her away, then running – but in reality nobody was there. Just him.

The screen went black and Monica saw that Sean had jumped up and grabbed the remote. He threw it down on the bed, animated now.

"Look, I've had enough of this. I want some answers."

The barman shot her a glance, but Monica didn't react to Sean's change of mood with so much as a tremor. It was important not to. She wanted the realisation, the epiphany, to come from within, not for the blame to rebound on her as the catalyst, which was why she had to be careful. This wasn't shooting a stag – the lobotomy approach – this was catching a butterfly and, with luck, setting it free. Psychologically at least.

She opened her folder and took out a set of ten-by-eight black and white photographs. "I'm going to show you some photographs, Sean, and I want you to tell me if you recognise who they are."

She placed the first photograph on the bed.

"The WPC, the policewoman who came first," he said. To the next photograph, equally easy: "The twins' mother." Next came the infamous, predatory woman in the wedding dress. "Yeah. The inebriated bird – what is this?"

Monica smiled. "Indulge me."

She laid down the next ten-by-eight.

"The woman Detective Inspector," said Sean, exasperatedly. "…you know this." Without pausing, Monica placed down next a photograph of Alison, Sean's wife. He looked away. "Ha ha, very unfunny."

Next, a photograph of a man.

Sean looked. "I don't know his name. Detective Sergeant something. OK. Time's up. What's going on here?"

Monica sat carefully back in her chair and looked at him with the fingers of one hand entwined in those of her other.

"Where do you think you are, Sean?"

"Where do I *think* I am? I'm in a country house hotel. What are you talking about?"

"You're in a hospital, Sean. A secure psychiatric hospital."

He shook his head with laughter. "You're bloody mad. There's nothing wrong with me. There's something bloody wrong with *you!*"

Monica didn't uncross her legs. "You had a breakdown, Sean. A total collapse. It started even before the trial."

"Trial?"

"It was a reaction to what you did. But I happen to think you're on the point of recovery."

"*Recovery?* Recovery from what?"

"Denial. A denial so complete as to lose contact with reality." She walked to the mirror, touched her own reflection. "Mental dissociation. You constructed in your mind a double – we call it an *eidolon* – as a distancing mechanism in order to psychologically cope with the enormity of your crimes."

Sean wanted to yell at her now. Derision wasn't enough, wasn't nearly enough. "Enormity...? What *crimes?*"

"About five years ago there began a series of fatal attacks on women in the North London area." She placed a cover of the Evening Standard on the coffee table between them. "The police had trouble catching him. It was down to fingerprints in the end. And DNA." Fingerprints? DNA? "A man randomly targeting and killing prostitutes. Brutally." She walked over to the bed and pointed to the photograph of the woman he had identified as the WPC. "Victim number one. Rachel Benn."

"This is a wind-up. All right, nice one."

She pointed to the photograph of the twins' mother. "Victim two. Eve Wagner." She pointed to the photograph of the drunken bride. "Victim three. Vivienne Hulk. Like the others, sexually assaulted. Mutilated. Her head…"

"Crap. Absolute bullshit."

She ignored his interjection and indicated the print of the Woman DI. "Victim four. Margaret Cobb. The same M.O. exactly." She pointed at the photograph of Ali, and as the acid rose in his throat and before he could say, *No, don't*, she was saying: "Victim five. Alison Hind."

Ali?

"His last victim. A mistake. The only one not a prostitute. She was a junior school teacher." Monica tugged the picture of the Detective Sergeant on top of it. "With a husband. Who came to the Old Bailey and stared you in the eye every day for five months. Do you remember him now?" She watched Sean stare down expressionlessly at the row of photographs. "A happily married wife and mother of two daughters…" *How are you, kids?* "Hannah and Polly…"

"Get – get out of here!"

Sean scooped up the photographs and threw them at the wall. The barman stepped forward ready to restrain him but Monica put a hand to his chest, signalling him to back off.

"A man was arrested, Sean. Unmarried. A loner. No family. No fixed abode. The only time anyone saw him was playing snooker at his local boozer. Man with a record of violence against – "

Sean covered his ears, didn't look at the new photograph in her hand.

"No. No! *NO!* SHUT UP! *SHUT UP!*"

He upturned the coffee table with the tabloid cover on. He tried to circle the room, but Monica stayed with him, right in his personal space. He couldn't shake her off. He picked up the newspaper and tore it into little pieces.

"Don't fight it, Sean. I'm trying to help you."

"You're *lying* to me!" He threw the pieces into her face.

"You needed to cope. You needed to escape. Your mind provided the answer. By splitting you into two different selves." She cornered Sean. He couldn't get past her. He couldn't escape. He slid down the wall. *Leave me alone. Leave me alone!* But she didn't leave him alone. She couldn't. This was it. This was what he had to hear. This was what he had to accept. "And what did you do? You created a happily married man, the total opposite of the lonely, disturbed, friendless, violent man you really were, and really hated. You created an identity you craved to be – *prayed* to be, even."

Sean moaned. He had his arms wrapped over his head now. He was rocking, sobbing. "No! No! It was *him!* It was HIM!"

She took his hands in hers, unwrapping them from his head, from his mind.

"The double you were afraid of was the real you. That's why he was trying to come through, that's why he was trying to take over. But that's *good!* Because when you can accommodate him, let him back in, when you can acknowledge the responsibility – then we can help you. Then you can get better."

"NOOOOOOOOOO!"

Sean couldn't take it. He started to sob uncontrollably.

I n the observation room, behind the mirror, Dr Paul Davenish, in pullover and cords, was murmuring to *himself: "He's not ready. He isn't sodding ready for it, chicken."*

Monica crouched up close to the shape of Sean, huddled foetus-like against the wall with his arms over his head. Now her voice was hushed and soothing:

"It was a fantasy. A fantasy wife. A fantasy *life*, Sean. Come back to reality. You can do it. I know you can."

The room was still and silent. Sean didn't move.

"Sean? Sean?"

She stood up and stepped back from him, proud of the fact that she hadn't touched him, even though she was tempted, and he needed it. But what he needed wasn't the same as what was good for his mental health and that was her call and nobody else's. Responsibility was the key. And if he turned that key, that was everything.

She sat on the bed, her flat hands sandwiched between her bony knees.

Suddenly aware of the bird song again, Sean uncurled from a ball. He sat still for a few minutes. *Ornithology.* Trees. The smell of new mown grass, et cetera. His senses began to wake each other up. He didn't ache any more, and the insides of his brain didn't slough around like dregs at the bottom of a bottle. That birdsong was remarkably sweet and the day seemed dainty and full of possibilities.

He stood up straight, wiping away tears with the balls of his thumbs. He'd let it all flow out, the dam had burst and he felt refreshed and renewed and reinvigorated.

Monica walked over to him. She delved into her pocket and took out the pack of Marlboro and lit up. It was sandpaper-like on the back of her throat because she didn't smoke that much, only on special occasions, but this was a special occasion. Nervously, pointedly, she offered him one.

He took it from her between finger and thumb. Considered it as a chimp might, sniffed it even, then reached out and put it neatly back in the packet.

"No thanks. I don't smoke."

He got up, smoothing the front of his trousers, and walked past her, as if on automatic pilot. As if he had only just woken up. As if the crusts of sleep were still in the corners of his eyes. He combed his hair in the mirror until it was presentably neat. It was like she wasn't in the room any more, and without looking back at her, he opened the door and walked out.

Breakfast was from seven thirty to nine and he was one of these people – it was one of the treats of coming away, wasn't it? – you don't want to miss the *breakfast*, do you? He found a jaunty spring returning to his step as he left his room and headed for the staircase, and began to whistle "The Girl from Ipanema". Maybe it was the sunlight through the stained glass. Maybe it was just the mood he was in after a good night's kip. Whatever it was, this morning he felt the stately hominess reassuring, the sense of family and history wrapping him up like a nice warm blanket. Even the paintings, the oil portraits from the time of Dr Dee or Dr Johnson, or both, seemed to look down more benevolently now. It was always a bit worrying booking a place sight unseen, but now he'd settled in, Shewstone House Hotel was somewhere he felt really at home. The food was good, the service was good, the rooms were good, the staff were friendly and hospitable. In fact, he didn't have a bad word to say about the place. He wondered why it wasn't publicised more, or was it one of those hideaways that people who stayed preferred to keep a closely guarded secret?

Descending the grand staircase, he nodded hello to the Prof Dumbledore lookalike and his Germaine Greer wife. He thought he might strike up a conversation with them later, maybe they weren't as fuddy-duddy as they looked. He might be a nuclear physicist and she a society madam. They could be a laugh. Giles gave him a little salute of recognition and Sean smiled back, hopping down the last few steps with Fred Astaire lightness.

The linen of breakfast shone in the glow from the windows. The restaurant was peppered with guests and waitresses. Sean sidestepped one, right, left, Laurel and Hardy fashion, laughing apologetically, and skipped to the table by the bay window.

Ali sipped her tea as she ran her eyes down the menu card. Sean joined her, unfolded his napkin and lay it across his lap, and poured himself a cup of tea from the pot.

"What happened to you?" she mumbled. "And they talk about women in the bathroom. Continental or full English? That's a silly question."

"Black pudding. Fried bread. Double egg, double sausage. The full Monty."

"The full heart attack."

"I'm on holiday. We're here to enjoy ourselves, remember. Remember?"

Ali arched an eyebrow. "Mmm. I've noticed."

He knew what was going through her mind. It was the exceedingly good sex they'd had the night before. He wasn't about to disagree. He had a smile on him like Zippy from *Rainbow,* too. She touched his hand, which was flat on the tablecloth, then he took hers and squeezed it.

"I love you," said Sean.

"I love you too, fat face," said his wife, reaching over to touch his cheek. He felt his stubble stand on end. It was nice that your wife could still do that for you. A voluminous Jamaican waitress asked if they wanted more tea and they said they did, please, and some toast while they were thinking what to order, if that was all right. Half white, half brown. That would be fabulous.

"Look. It's a beautiful morning," said Ali.

"I know."

"I feel as if we've been away forever already. That's the great thing. And the whole weekend stretches ahead of us."

"It does," said Sean. "This is only our first day. This is just the beginning." He leant over and, not caring who was watching, kissed her on the lips.

Acknowledgements

Thanks to everyone who has had input in this project or otherwise helped along the way: Ruth Baumgarten, James Saynor, Foz Allan, Peter Engelmann, Steven Lockley, Charlie Hey and, last but not least, "Professor" Gary Fry.

Stephen Volk
Bradford-on-Avon
July 2009

Other books from Gray Friar Press

Poe's Progeny – An Anthology of Contemporary Stories Inspired by Classic Dark Fiction
- 30 original tales from the modern masters of horror

Bernie Herrmann's Manic Sextet
- Six original novelettes

The Faculty of Terror by John L Probert
- A sublime film horror anthology in prose

Dark Corners by Stephen Volk
- A collection of stories from the *Ghostwatch* author

Stains by Paul Finch
- Novellas and short stories from a master of horror

Dirty Prayers by Gary McMahon
- 25 short stories from a powerful new voice in horror

Rain by Conrad Williams
- A devastating novella

Hard Roads by Steve Vernon
- Two wild novellas set in Canada

The Appetite by Nicholas Royle
- A powerful novella set in contemporary London.

Passport to Purgatory by Tony Richards
- Tales of terror from around the world

The Impelled and Other Head Trips by Gary Fry
- Reissue of the classic first collection

The Catacombs of Fear by John Llewellyn Probert
- Another Amicus-style horror anthology

Mindful of Phantoms by Gary Fry
- 18 terrifying supernatural short stories

Pictures of the Dark by Simon Bestwick
- Stunningly dark short stories and novelettes

Groaning Shadows by Paul Finch
- Four masterful horror novellas

Many more exciting projects on the horizon at
www.grayfriarpress.com

Lightning Source UK Ltd.
Milton Keynes UK
16 October 2009

145033UK00001B/4/P

9 781906 331146